Sugar Spinelli's
Little Instruction Book

I can't believe my eyes! Look over there, Theda. Isn't that Melissa Bright? I heard tell she lost her fiancé not long ago. And her in the family way, too, bless her heart. What do you suppose she's doing here? Oh, my Lord! It looks like she's planning to buy her baby a new daddy. I don't know what the world's coming to. Even if Melissa's pretty enough to get that cowboy to hang around for a few days, forever's going to cost her a whole lot more....

D1040808

Dear Reader,

We just knew you wouldn't want to miss the news event that has all of Wyoming abuzz! There's a herd of eligible bachelors on their way to Lightning Creek—and they're all for sale!

Cowboy, park ranger, rancher, P.I.—they all grew up at Lost Springs Ranch, and every one of these mavericks has his price, so long as the money's going to help keep Lost Springs afloat.

The auction is about to begin! Young and old, every woman in the state wants in on the action, so pony up some cash and join the fun. The man of your dreams might just be up for grabs!

Marsha Zinberg
Editorial Coordinator, HEART OF THE WEST

Rent-A-Dad
Judy Christenberry

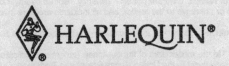

HARLEQUIN®

TORONTO • NEW YORK • LONDON
AMSTERDAM • PARIS • SYDNEY • HAMBURG
STOCKHOLM • ATHENS • TOKYO • MILAN • MADRID
PRAGUE • WARSAW • BUDAPEST • AUCKLAND

Judy Christenberry is acknowledged as the author of this work.

ISBN 0-373-82595-1

RENT-A-DAD

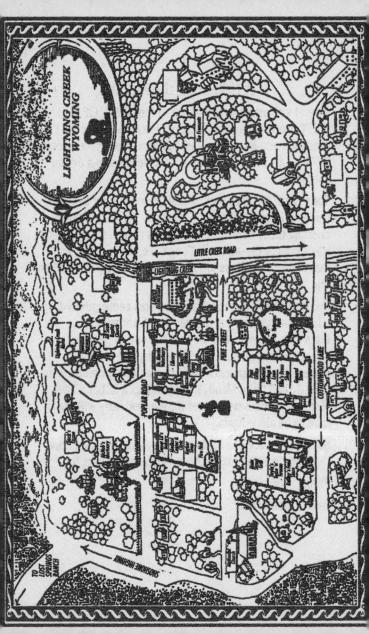

A Note from the Author

When I was asked to contribute to the HEART OF THE WEST continuity series, I was really excited. After all, I'd read Montana Mavericks, Delta Justice and Crystal Creek. To be a part of one of these special series was a dream come true.

Then came the hard part...which turned out not to be so bad at all! I had to write the book. But I had such fun creating these characters that giving them a happy ending was a pleasure—and a challenge. We, the readers, know that Melissa and Russ belong together. But try telling them that....

I've discovered that most of my stories center around a family—building one, finding one, living with one. I'm a firm believer that the family is one of the most important things in life. So it's no surprise that those close relationships once again play a predominant role in *Rent-A-Dad*. Little Mandy will never lack a father's love. Melissa gains a sexy partner for life. And Russ will never have to be alone again.

So, for the price of a bachelor, everybody's happy. I hope that once you've finished *Rent-A-Dad*, you will be, too.

Enjoy,

Judy Christenberry

This book is dedicated to my dear friend Barbara Harrison, who cheers me on, no matter what, and offers a shoulder to cry on when I need it. Thanks, Barbara, for always being there for me.

PROLOGUE

"ARE YOU SURE I SHOULD dress as a cowboy?" Russ Hall surveyed himself in the mirror, noting the tight jeans, boots, leather vest and work shirt. "I'm an architect now."

Lindsay Duncan stared at him assessingly. "Well, I suppose we could dress you as a construction worker, but—"

"Never mind." What difference did it make? He might be an architect now, but he'd spent enough time as a kid chasing cows. He felt comfortable in these clothes.

And if dressing like a cowboy made more money for the Lost Springs Ranch for Boys, it was the least he could do. After all, he owed just about everything he had to Lost Springs. The ranch had become his home at the age of four, when his mother had abandoned him.

If it weren't for that, no way in hell would he go through with this bachelor auction business. But the ranch's finances were at an all-time low, and Russ would do whatever he could to help, even if that meant being sold to the highest bidder. At least it was only for a weekend.

Most disturbing of all were the memories that had flooded him on his return to Wyoming. Once he'd gotten a scholarship and gone to Chicago, he'd never come back to Lost Springs.

"I'm so glad you're here, Russ," Lindsay said, patting his shoulder. The two of them had stayed close friends. Lindsay's parents had operated the ranch until their death a few yeas ago, and now Lindsay herself was in charge.

Guilt filled Russ. When he left the ranch, he'd wanted to put his past behind him. Memories of his mother and her abandonment were too disturbing to confront. "Sorry, Lindsay. Guess I got involved in my career." He smiled at her. It did feel good to see her.

Maybe the time was right to come back to Wyoming. When he'd stepped off the plane two days ago, a strange feeling of homecoming had filled him. A feeling he had difficulty recognizing because he didn't really have a home. Certainly not his sterile condo in Chicago.

"Just one more thing," Lindsay added, stepping closer.

Before Russ knew what was happening, she'd undone all but the last button on his shirt.

"Hey!" he protested. "What are you doing?"

"Showcasing your sex appeal," she said with a grin. "We'll make more money that way."

You're doing this to make money, Russ reminded himself. *This is for the ranch.* But he suddenly felt like a hunk of cheese set out for the mice.

MELISSA BRIGHT QUESTIONED her sanity. What was she doing at a bachelor auction? Was she crazy? She stared down at the list she'd made a few minutes ago, waiting for the auction to begin. All the logical reasons for her attending the auction were there.

Publicity for her business, a donation for the ranch, the chance to help out a friend. She'd met Lindsay Duncan, the owner of Lost Springs Ranch, through Melissa's fiancé, Greg, and they'd become fast friends. That friendship had deepened with their mutual mourning after Greg's death in a traffic accident over four months ago.

Before that time, she and Greg had discussed using the auction to gain publicity for her greeting card business. Bidding on a bachelor to model for her cards would not only help her fledgling company but benefit the ranch, as well. Greg had even teased her about falling for one of the hunks.

There was no chance of that. Her heart had belonged to Greg and still did. A kinder, gentler man had not existed, making his untimely death impossible to accept.

She eyed some of the women around her as they whispered among themselves. Most were dressed casually in jeans and vests, although some had gone all out for the occasion. The redhead next to her wore a revealing scarlet cocktail dress. She certainly wanted to draw attention to herself.

Melissa looked down at her conservative navy-blue suit. She sure couldn't compete with the other woman's plunging neckline.

Taped music suddenly filled the air, alerting the audience that the auction was about to start. Lindsay stepped on stage to welcome the crowd packing the bleachers, and Melissa drew a shaky breath.

"Ladies and gentlemen, thank you so much for joining us today," Lindsay began.

Melissa stared at the paper in her hand, trying to concentrate on her list.

"—volunteered their services for a fantasy weekend of the woman's choice—"

Melissa sighed. She hoped her "hunk" wouldn't be upset with her plans. They hardly qualified as fantasy.

"Let the bachelor auction begin!" Lindsay finished to rousing applause.

Melissa drew a deep breath. She wasn't sure what she was looking for. Someone who would draw publicity for her company, first of all. She nibbled her bottom lip as the auctioneer introduced the first bachelor.

The women around her went wild when the sexy man took Lindsay's hand and lifted it to his lips for a courtly kiss. He was a doctor, and breathtakingly handsome, but Melissa was more entertained by the behavior of the women around her. There was such exuberance and enjoyment of life in their rowdiness that it made her own spirits lift.

Sometime later, a cowboy stepped up to the stage. Tall, muscular, he was dressed in western clothes, his shirt unbuttoned down his admittedly magnificent chest. What on earth would she do with a cowboy?

Suddenly she lifted her arm in the air. Of course! A sexy cowboy would be the perfect prototype for her line of greeting cards.

WHEN RUSS HEARD THE WORD *sold,* he grinned. He'd brought a good price. His smile disappeared when the woman who'd purchased him stood to go pay for her bid.

She was pregnant.

He hurried off the stage, his gaze zeroing in on his old friend Lindsay. "What's going on?" he demanded.

"You did great!" Lindsay assured him. Then she turned to the next bachelor.

"That's not what I mean, Lindsay. The woman's pregnant. How am I supposed to romance a pregnant woman?"

"She's pregnant?" Lindsay asked, spinning around to face him. "Did she have dark hair?"

"Yeah, with sad brown eyes. You know her?"

"Oh, Russ, it's my friend Melissa. Don't worry, she's not looking for romance. She's going to use you as a model for her business, if you agree, and for publicity."

"Of course I'll agree. She's paying. But—"

"Don't worry," Lindsay interrupted him. "You'll like her. She's very sweet."

Sweet? Russ stood there in shock as Lindsay was summoned by someone outside the arena.

Sweet? He'd figured he'd be with someone fun, interesting, enticing. Maybe even hot. But sweet?

He equated sweet with boring. He worried the sweet lady who'd just purchased a weekend of his time would make him want to give up women entirely.

CHAPTER ONE

Almost one year later

RUSS HALL SCANNED his mail as he removed his suit coat. When the postmark from Wyoming caught his eye, he paused. He didn't correspond with many friends in his home state. And if he did, they sent their correspondence to his high-rise apartment, not the office.

He opened the envelope and pulled out a sheet of paper. After scanning it, he sat in his desk chair and reread it carefully.

Damn. The lady was calling in her chips. That auction he'd participated in last June was finally coming home to roost. The bachelor weekends were supposed to be redeemed within one year, and the lady with the sad eyes was slipping just under the wire.

He'd thought about her the past year...more than he'd expected. He remembered Lindsay saying something about him modeling for the woman's company. He'd forgotten what kind of company it was. Suddenly he wondered if he was going to be asked to do something...erotic. No, he instantly dismissed that idea. Lindsay had described the woman as sweet. Sweet and erotic didn't match up. Sweet and pregnant definitely didn't point in that direction.

Another thought occurred to him. When he'd returned to Wyoming for the auction, he'd been surprised by the sense of satisfaction that had filled him. While there, he'd even considered relocating permanently. Then, when he'd flown back to Chicago, he'd gotten caught up in the demands of his job and forgotten all about it.

But there'd been an edge of restlessness since his trip last summer. He'd shoved it aside, tried to pretend everything was all right.

Maybe he'd been waiting until he *had* to return to Wyoming once again. Maybe while he was there, fulfilling the terms of the auction, he'd think about moving back once more. Going home...

"OH, MANDY, NO!" Melissa protested just before her box of dusting powder hit the bathroom floor. Mandy, seven months old, blinked in surprise. Then her face contorted into the saddest look in creation and big tears rolled down her baby cheeks.

"Don't cry, sweetie. It's Mommy's fault for leaving it on the side of the tub." Melissa gathered her daughter in her arms, dusting off the powder that had splashed on Mandy. "Besides," she added with a laugh, "it makes you smell good."

With determination, she walked away from the mess. She didn't have time to clean it up. Her guest's plane was due at the Casper airport in half an hour and she didn't want to be late. After all, this was Mandy's Mother's Day gift to her.

Last June, when she'd bid on the bachelor, she'd only been thinking in terms of using him for her greeting card company, Wyoming Bright. But after seven months as a single mom, Melissa had decided she could use a break.

And what better time than Mother's Day?

She was going to turn the sexy bachelor into a glorified baby-sitter for just one morning so she could sleep past sunrise. That was going to be her baby's gift to her.

One glorious morning of uninterrupted sleep.

Not that she would leave her precious child to the care of someone she didn't know. She was staying put the entire weekend. She wasn't foolish enough to think a single architect from Chicago would know anything about baby care. But she would teach him. Even just one morning of sleeping in would be worth it.

Oh, the heaven of that thought stopped her in her tracks.

She wasn't a morning person, but Mandy was. She and the sun got up every morning at six o'clock. Melissa hoped that by Sunday her sexy bachelor would have convinced her he could care for Mandy long enough to let her mommy sleep in.

"What a waste of testosterone!" Melissa said out loud, giggling at the thought.

Mandy patted her cheek and cooed.

Smiling at her baby, Melissa sent up a silent prayer

of gratitude. Yes, they were happy. She'd recovered from the death of Mandy's father. The pain was still there, but it was bearable, and she'd learned to laugh again for the sake of her child.

She only had one thing left to deal with from that desolate period of her life: Mr. Bachelor. She had a lot of ideas for him, though the main one was relief from twenty-four-hour parenting duties. It probably wasn't exactly what he'd expected when he'd volunteered for the auction, but she sure hoped he had a sympathetic nature—and a sense of humor.

If he was agreeable, she also wanted to take some photos of him in his cowboy garb. Some of her greeting cards were drawn, but more and more, the public seemed to like photographs. She envisioned a hunky cowboy in an old bathtub, his chest naked above the water. Maybe that idea had been inspired by the cowboy's open shirt at the auction.

She shrugged aside the erotic appeal. *She* wasn't interested in the man's physical attributes, but if they sold more cards, she wouldn't object. But would he?

Somehow, she wasn't even sure she'd have the nerve to ask him to pose. She'd thought about offering to pay him for his services. But he was a successful architect. Probably, he would refuse.

Raising her chin, she stared sightlessly at the wall. She'd faced challenges before. Her parents had died within a week of each other of a rare viral infection her senior year in college. For months, she'd spun out of control, unable to make a decision, unsure where to turn.

Then she'd found Greg. He'd been her anchor. He might not have been the hunk those bachelors were, but he'd been the center of her universe. He'd made her whole.

Then he'd died, too.

But she hadn't let go of his guidance. It had been Greg's suggestion to purchase a bachelor. He had been the one who had convinced her the card company would eventually be a success. And Greg had believed she could be a good parent.

She was trying.

Somehow, she'd find a way to use this weekend to her advantage.

"Let's go collect our cowboy, okay, Mandy? And then we'll turn him into a houseboy. What fun!"

RUSS FROWNED AS HE ENTERED the airport. The flight had seemed interminable. His seatmate had been a young woman with a baby who cried most of the trip. He'd asked the flight attendant if he could move, but the flight was fully booked.

Now he had a raging headache.

Disgruntled, he looked around for the woman who had clung to his memories for almost a year. His gaze passed over a brunette holding a baby, then flashed back as he realized she also held a sign. With his name on it.

How stupid of him. Somehow he'd expected her to still be pregnant, frozen in time, but that was ridiculous. It had been ten months since the auction and she'd been showing then.

"Mr. Hall?" she said, her beautiful voice rising in expectation.

The mysterious Ms. Bright. The bachelors had been asked to provide a luxurious weekend for their purchaser. Although it was ladies' choice, Russ had been prepared to offer a weekend in Chicago, tickets to see the Bulls, museum tours, whatever Ms. Bright desired.

Instead, he'd been informed that his buyer had already decided on the particulars for the weekend. He supposed that included the modeling Lindsay had referred to, though it wasn't mentioned in the letter he'd received. Ms. Bright's only request had been that he bring a swimsuit. He'd packed both formal and informal clothing and hoped for the best. But now, as he stared at the baby smiling at him, he got an uneasy feeling in his stomach.

At least this baby wasn't crying.

"You must be Melissa Bright," he said.

"Yes. Welcome to Wyoming."

He nodded, then stood there, waiting for her to direct him. After all, she was supposed to be in charge.

"Do you have more luggage?" she asked, indicating his garment bag and grip.

He raised his eyebrows. She expected a clothes-horse? "No, ma'am. I travel light."

She led the way out of the airport building to her car, a compact that didn't have much leg room. He stowed his bags in the trunk, then moved to the passenger seat while Melissa settled the baby in a car seat in back.

With a grimace, he drew his knees up close and fastened the seat belt.

"Sorry you're crowded," she apologized as she slid behind the wheel. "I'd forgotten that you're so tall."

It rankled a bit that she hadn't remembered him when he'd been haunted by those sad eyes. With a frown, he realized they weren't sad anymore. Her dark-brown gaze seemed to have dancing lights in it.

"I remembered you as sad," he said abruptly, then regretted his words.

She shot him a startled look, then turned away, starting the car. "You won't be uncomfortable long. It's not far to the house."

She'd completely ignored his remark. Okay. Hoping for a little more room, he eased back against the seat. As a boy, he'd been tall for his age. He was used to being crowded. He'd used his height to his advantage, though, and still did. Women were attracted to tall men.

The gurgling sound of the baby distracted him, and he asked, "Where's your husband, and how does he feel about you buying a bachelor?"

Again she seemed taken aback, but at least she answered this time. "He's dead. And we were never married."

Now it was his turn to be shocked. "I'm sorry." What else could he say?

"Thanks." Then she shot him a smile. "How was your flight?"

She was obviously making an effort to be cheerful, but she'd chosen the wrong question. "Miserable. A young woman with a baby sat next to me. The baby cried the entire flight."

She skipped all the obvious comments. "You don't like babies?"

"I didn't say that."

"It was in your voice."

He released a weary sigh. "Look, Melissa, how I feel about babies doesn't make a hill-of-beans difference to our agreement. But if you'd been closed up in a plane with a screaming kid beside you, you might feel the same way."

"Mandy had colic the first three months. Well, actually almost four months. Do you know what that's like, Mr. Hall? It's like your airplane flight times one hundred."

He moaned, just the thought making his headache worse.

"Are you ill?"

"I'm fine," he snapped. "As soon as we reach our destination, I'll take something for this headache. In the morning, I'll be perfectly recovered and ready for whatever you've planned for the next three days."

Another quick glance before she looked away. "Good."

"Exactly what have you planned?"

"Um, nothing elaborate."

Had she changed her mind about the modeling? There went the tux he'd packed. At a little over six three, he couldn't count on finding a rental that fit. "Could you be a little more specific?"

"I could, but you might want to wait until after you've taken something for your headache."

He stared in fascination as the corner of her mouth turned up slightly.

About to ask her what was so amusing, he stopped when she spoke first.

"Are you familiar with Casper?"

"Yeah. Growing up on the ranch, we boys competed for the privilege to come to the big city. We thought Casper was the most sophisticated place in the world."

She smiled. "I guess Chicago's a little bigger and a lot more sophisticated, huh?"

"Oh, yeah. Ever been there?"

"No. I grew up in Casper. I've been to Denver a few times, and, of course, Cheyenne, but that's about the extent of my travels."

"You could've spent a long weekend in Chicago if you wanted," he reminded her. Then he would have been in control of the situation, something he preferred when it came to women.

Mandy's squeal reminded him of why that might've been a problem.

"Just a minute, sweetie," Melissa called over her shoulder. "Would you look for her pacifier? I think she may have thrown it down."

Russ gingerly turned in his seat as far as the seat

belt allowed and looked at the baby. The pacifier was caught between her round tummy and the guardrail of the baby seat. Reaching back, he plucked it up, then stared at the baby as she gurgled and clapped her hands.

"What do I do now?" he asked.

"You found it? Just put it back in her mouth."

With a frown, he stretched a little more and offered the pacifier to the baby. Expecting to have to urge her to take the thing, he was surprised when she leaned forward, took the pacifier in her mouth and held it there with both hands.

"She took it!"

One eyebrow shot up over those warm brown eyes. "Of course she did."

Russ settled back into his seat, annoyed by her superior tones.

"I haven't been around babies much."

"Yes, I guessed that," she said with a sigh. As if it mattered to her.

Tough. If she'd wanted a man experienced with children, she shouldn't have sought out a bachelor.

She turned into a side street, a quiet, residential area with small, neatly kept homes. When she pulled into the third driveway and stopped the car, he didn't move.

"What are we doing?"

"This is where Mandy and I live, Russ."

"I'm spending the weekend here?"

"Yes. Sorry if you were hoping for something more exotic."

"Look, I'm happy to cover the expenses of the weekend. I'll be glad to pay for a hotel if you—"

"No, thank you," she said before he could finish, her tone crisp. "If you can't handle staying here, you're welcome to go to a hotel, but it will be inconvenient for what I have in mind."

"I didn't mean to offend you but—that's what I need to know. What *do* you have in mind?"

She looked away. "Let's get you comfortable first, then we'll talk about the weekend."

This stalling was making him uneasy. Which didn't help his headache. But her request wasn't unreasonable. Hell, some people might even say it was kind. The way his head was throbbing, he shouldn't complain.

He gathered his luggage from the trunk as she released the baby from her car seat. Then he followed the two of them to the front door. She juggled the baby and the keys with practiced ease and swung open the door.

Following her in, he discovered a casual living room that shouted the word *home*. Two comfortable flowered couches made an L-shape in front of the fireplace. Over to the side was a large green leather chair with an ottoman in front of it, picking up the green on the couches.

He almost made a beeline for the chair, then caught himself. He couldn't settle in for a rest, as his head pleaded. He wasn't at home. Instead, he was a guest and had to behave politely.

She must have been a mind reader.

"Why don't you put your luggage down and sit over there," she said, waving to the green chair. "I'll find some Tylenol and put dinner on the table. You'll feel better after you've eaten."

He didn't hesitate this time. Throwing his bags on the end of the nearest sofa, he sank down into the soft leather, closing his eyes and sighing in pleasure.

MELISSA STARED at the large male practically passed out in her living room. She remembered when she'd first seen him. It had been a terrible time in her life. She'd been pregnant with her dead fiancé's child, mourning Greg and confused about everything.

She'd chosen Russ because he would benefit her company. But she'd also found him surprisingly appealing. It was only because he was dressed as a cowboy, she told herself. After all, she was living in Wyoming.

But many months had passed before she'd decided what to do with the sexy bachelor. Late one night, rocking her colicky baby, her eyelids drooping shut, she decided his best use would be to give her a complete night's rest. To let her sleep in at least one morning. She'd already paid for him, after all.

Looking at him now, she shook her head in self-derision. This wasn't going to work. Anyone with a brain the size of a pea could see that.

He didn't like babies.

And, much to her surprise, he was sexy enough to arouse emotions in her that she thought she'd buried with her fiancé. With effort, she jerked her gaze away from his long, lean body.

Curiously, she wondered if her idea of turning Russ into a nursemaid had been her way of dealing with a sexy man in her life for three whole days. She stared at him again. Somehow, the image of Russ with a bottle in one hand and a diaper in the other didn't diminish his sexiness one little bit.

Cuddling Mandy against her with a sigh, she headed for the kitchen. She'd done most of the preparations for dinner earlier in the afternoon. She'd figured he should have a good meal before she told him about her plans.

"In you go, sweetie," she said as she settled Mandy in her high chair. She put a teething biscuit on the tray to appease the baby while she finished dinner.

A few minutes later, she set some Tylenol beside Russ's plate before she called him to dinner.

He joined her in the small dining room, the perpetual frown he'd worn since his arrival eased somewhat.

"This looks good," he said politely.

"Thank you." It should. She'd cooked a pot roast, the prime beef nestled in a ring of carrots and potatoes, along with a tossed salad and green beans. Hot rolls were wrapped in a blue napkin in a woven basket, and a home-baked apple pie sat on the kitchen counter.

He waited until she was seated before he joined

her. Then he asked, touching the bottle of pain reliever, "May I?"

Such excessive consideration surprised her.

"Yes, of course."

Half an hour later, after her guest had consumed his last bite of apple pie, he leaned back in his seat.

"Melissa, that was a wonderful dinner. But I'm beginning to feel like a condemned man enjoying his last meal. I think it's time you told me exactly what it is you have in mind."

CHAPTER TWO

RUSS FELT THE TENSION rise in him again as his hostess stared across the table, her brown eyes wide. When she still said nothing, he urged, "Melissa?"

"Yes, well…" She paused, nibbling on her full bottom lip, and an unexpected surge of desire hit him.

He caught himself glaring at the woman. What was wrong with her? He'd offered a fun-filled weekend and she'd rejected it, bringing him to her home instead. She wasn't supposed to be so appealing. According to Lindsay, she'd bought him for business purposes.

She cleared her throat. "I think maybe I've made a mistake."

"A mistake?" he parroted. "I don't understand."

"Um, well, when I purchased you—I mean, your weekend, I did so because you would be perfect publicity for my company. I have a greeting card company. But then, later, when—when—never mind. It won't work. I'll take you to a hotel for tonight, and tomorrow you can return to Chicago."

He should have been pleased. To his surprise, he wasn't. "I keep my promises, Melissa. You paid a lot for this weekend. Are you going to ask for your money back?''

''Of course not! I would never do that to Lindsay.''

''You and Lindsay are friends?''

''Yes. I understand you know each other well.''

''I grew up at the ranch. It was my home for fourteen years. Lindsay's a bit younger, but of course we're friends.''

Though his hostess smiled, her attention was directed to her baby daughter, who was chewing contentedly on a teething biscuit.

Melissa turned to look at him again. ''Lindsay's great. And the auction was a complete success.''

''Yes, it was. So what did you have in mind for me?'' he asked, not willing to let her escape.

She sent him a winsome smile, one that lit up her brown eyes and showed off her white, even teeth. ''It was a silly idea. Perhaps you'd like to stay the weekend in Casper, look up old friends, spend some time out at the ranch?''

''That sounds pleasant,'' he assured her, more determined than ever to find out what she'd planned. ''Unfortunately, the weekend isn't supposed to please me. Lindsay said you wanted me to do some modeling.''

''Yes, but I came up with another idea, and I can assure you, Mr. Hall, what I planned wouldn't please you at all.'' Her smile widened. ''It was a crazy idea, one that came to me one night about two in the morning when I was trying to get Mandy to sleep.''

"Two in the morning? She keeps late hours."

"You don't know the half of it," Melissa muttered.

"So what occurred to you at two in the morning?"

She shrugged her shoulders. "A Mother's Day present."

Mother's Day wasn't a special day for him. His own mother had abandoned him. As long as Mrs. Duncan, Lindsay's mother, had been alive, he'd sent her flowers or a gift. But it wasn't his favorite holiday.

"You mean a special night out? I have no problem with that. Casper has some good restaurants. We could—"

"No." She stopped him, still smiling. "I don't want to go out."

Frustration was building, along with his headache. "Look, Melissa, I'm trying to be patient, but I'm beginning to feel like I'm back on that plane, trapped beside a screaming kid. Could you just tell me what you wanted?"

Melissa drew a deep breath and gave him an honest answer. "I wanted you to be me…at least for one morning."

She almost burst out laughing at the dumbfounded expression on his face. "It's all right. I realize I wasn't thinking straight."

"I don't even understand what you mean."

No, he wouldn't. No one would until they'd been given total responsibility for a baby with little support. "I don't have relatives here. I have a great-aunt in Denver. She's eighty-two. That's the extent of my family. My fiancé died a week before our wedding when I was already pregnant. It's just me and Mandy now."

He was watching her, still frowning. "And?"

"I love her to death, but she's up at six every morning." She sighed. "She sometimes doesn't even sleep through the night. I have my own company, which involves a lot of work. I haven't had enough sleep since she was born. At two in the morning, the thought of having someone else take over, even for one morning, and let me sleep in..." She almost groaned out loud. "That's what I thought of." She smiled wearily at him, knowing what he was going to say.

It was a stupid idea.

When he said nothing, she dared glance up at him. And almost burst into laughter again. "I know. You don't have to say it," she assured him. And as much as she'd like some help, she was relieved by the shocked expression on his face. Somehow, facing the real live man, rather than a distant memory, made her idea impossible. He was too...too good-looking to be a baby-sitter.

"You were going to turn your baby over to a complete stranger? A bachelor with no experience?"

"No! No, I was going to stay here with you, show you the routine, be here for Mandy. But I was going to sleep late...just one morning. Mother's Day. Sleep until I woke up, and just lie there, maybe have breakfast in bed." She sighed at the thought.

Dead silence followed.

Again she looked at her guest. The stunned expression was gone, replaced by a speculative stare that snapped her from her longings.

"I told you it was ridiculous. So, do you want to go back to Chicago tomorrow or spend the weekend visiting with friends?"

"Where am I supposed to sleep?"

His question threw her. "I beg your pardon?"

"I assume I'm supposed to stay here with you and Mandy, right? Otherwise I wouldn't be here when she woke up. Do you have a bedroom for me?"

She gulped. He was considering her idea? "Yes! Yes, you will—would sleep in the master bedroom. I have it all ready. But I can take you to a hotel. I'll pay for it, of course, since—"

He stood up and headed toward the living room, where he'd left his luggage. "I'll get my bags."

Her hope deflated. He was going to leave.

"Of course," she said. She wiped Mandy's sticky fingers and face and lifted her from the high chair. "Does it matter which hotel? I'll call and—"

He reappeared in the kitchen doorway. "I'm staying here."

RUSS WATCHED the various emotions that flickered across her face. Melissa had a very expressive face, one that drew a man in even when he had no intentions of responding. He'd watched her as she'd talked of her plan. A simple plan, really. Not asking for much. Just to sleep in one morning.

How could he resist such a plea?

Not that he knew a damn thing about babies, but if she was going to stay here, he could ask her questions. How difficult could it be?

"Here?" she squeaked, surprised.

"Here. We agreed on three days. Three days you get. But I'm warning you. I know nothing about babies."

A glowing smile spread over her face. "I'll show you. It's not that hard. Just don't leave her alone unless she's in her bed. She's even working on climbing out of the high chair."

"How old is she?" he asked in astonishment.

"Just over seven months. And already pulling herself up on things. Today she stood by the side of the tub and knocked off my bath powder. Oh. I didn't clean it up. I'll do that as soon as I show you where you'll sleep."

He could see the excitement rising in her, evidenced by her body language. He suddenly wondered if his own mother had simply grown too tired of the burden of raising a child by herself. It was the first thought he'd had of his mother in a long time that hadn't condemned her, and it took him by surprise.

"This way," she said as she walked down a short hall, Mandy on her hip. The baby watched him over her mother's arm, her brown eyes almost as big as Melissa's.

It was a small house. The bedroom, the master bedroom, wasn't large, but like the living room, it was pleasant, airy and welcoming. The queen-size bed was covered with a white goose-down comforter and big fluffy pillows, simple, not frilly.

He'd hoped for a king-size bed, but he shrugged his shoulders. He'd be comfortable here.

"I cleared space in the closet for your clothes, and I emptied two drawers in the dresser," she said.

He nodded, missing the meaning of her words. Then it struck him. "This is your room?"

"Yes, normally, but I'm sleeping—"

"I should take the guest room. You stay in here." He wasn't sure he'd be able to sleep, anyway, if he thought about her in the bed. More and more his eyes were drawn to her slender curves.

"Oh, no. That's impossible. I'm staying in my office."

"You said you were staying here," he reminded her sharply, panic flooding him at the idea of being on his own with a baby.

"My office here," she explained. "I have three bedrooms. Mandy's, this one and the third, which I turned into a home office. But there's a nice couch. I'm going to sleep on it."

It occurred to him again that this woman wasn't asking for all that much. She intended to sleep on a couch, giving him her comfortable bed, so she could sleep late one morning. The comforts he'd enjoyed since he'd taken his job in Chicago shamed him. He had life pretty easy compared to Melissa. He even had a maid to clean his apartment every week.

"I'll take the sofa bed," he assured her gruffly.

"No. You see, it's not a sofa bed and—well,

you're too big. It's much more my size.'' She smiled as if she'd won a prize. Then she took his garment bag from him and put it in the closet.

With a shake of his head, he followed and set his tote bag on the floor. She whisked around him and turned back the cover on the bed, revealing blue-and-white-striped sheets.

At least he wouldn't have to sleep on a lacy, flowery bed.

"The bathroom is the door at the end of the hall. I'll go sweep up the powder on the floor. Then it will be all yours while I put Mandy to bed. That usually takes a while," she finished with a rueful smile at her baby.

Mandy gurgled, as if agreeing with her mother.

"You only have one bathroom?" he asked before he realized how impolite his words sounded.

"Yes, but you can have first—you're right. This is never going to work." She turned back to the closet, lifting his garment bag from the rod.

His hand covered hers and forced the bag back onto the rod. The warmth of her, the soft floral scent she wore, enveloped him, and he rapidly withdrew his hand. "I'm sorry. I wasn't criticizing your home. I was surprised, that's all."

"I realize your place is probably more—more luxurious than mine, but—"

"Your home is nice and I'll be more than comfortable here. More than you will be."

She stared at him, seemingly unsure of what to do.

"Look, Russ, this is a mistake. We both know it.

Let me take you to a hotel. Whether you stay the weekend or go home at once is up to you.''

He squared his jaw and stared down at her. ''I'm not leaving.''

She slumped against the wall, obviously too tired to argue again. ''We'll talk in the morning.'' And she walked out of her bedroom.

RUSS UNPACKED HIS TWO BAGS, his mind racing. He'd talked to some of the other bachelors. They'd had interesting weekends that involved spending time with a sexy woman, often wining and dining her. Some had even ended in marriage.

His weekend was going to be a little different. He'd be offering formula to a seven-month-old. The baby's mother, though she certainly qualified as an attractive woman, had sleep, not sex on her mind.

But in spite of the opportunities she'd given him to walk away, he couldn't. Those big brown eyes would haunt him the rest of his life if he did. He wasn't normally considered a softy, but somehow Melissa got to him.

When he heard his hostess enter a room across from his, he opened his door. ''Are you putting her to bed now?'' he asked.

She spun around, as if he'd taken her by surprise. Then she turned her back to him. ''Yes, I am. We'll try not to disturb you.''

''I thought you might let me watch. So I'll know what to do.''

Again Melissa faced him, frowning. ''Russ, I told

you—'' But the baby rubbed her eye with a pudgy fist and whimpered, distracting her mother. Russ stepped across the hall while Melissa soothed her child.

"Is she all right?" he asked.

"Yes. She's tired. Come on, sweetie, let's put on your jammies and change your diaper." She placed the baby in her crib with a stuffed toy.

"Will she mind if I watch?" It seemed kind of intrusive to him to be so intimate with a stranger, even if the stranger was a baby.

His question, at least, erased that stiff expression Melissa had been wearing. With a chuckle, she shook her head. "No, she won't mind. A seven-month-old has no modesty at all."

He stood there as Melissa moved around the room, taking a disposable diaper from the top of the dresser, finding a clean sleeper from the top drawer.

"She wears that footy thing to bed? I thought she'd wear a nightgown," he said.

"She always throws off the covers," she told him. "With a sleeper, I know her feet are warm."

He leaned over the baby, lying in her crib. "You've got a good mommy, Mandy."

Mandy gurgled and rolled over, then pushed herself to a sitting position. Before he knew it, she'd pulled herself to a standing position, clinging to the railing of the crib.

"Hey! Look what she did," he exclaimed, amazed.

Melissa glanced over her shoulder. "That's why I

told you never to leave her alone, except when she's in her bed. I'm afraid she'll fall to the floor and break something.''

She came back to the baby's bed and settled Mandy onto the mattress again to change her diaper. Russ watched her carefully. Not that diapering a baby was difficult, but it was new territory for him. At the ranch, most of the boys were long past diapers.

Mandy smiled at him after Melissa removed the T-shirt she'd been wearing. He couldn't hold back a matching grin. ''She likes having her clothes changed?''

''No,'' Melissa said with a smile. ''I told you, she has no modesty. She likes to go without clothes at all.''

As if to prove her mother's point, Mandy tried to squirm away from Melissa as she slipped the sleeper onto her arms and legs. In spite of all her wriggling, the baby couldn't get free, and Melissa quickly did up the snaps. ''Mandy, behave,'' Melissa ordered, but her tone was soft.

''As soon as you turn out the light, will she pull it off again?'' he asked.

''No. She takes a bottle before bedtime, and it makes her too drowsy to think of it, even if she could undo the snaps.''

''So you're not breast-feeding her?'' he asked. One of his friends had become a father and talked about breast-feeding. Instantly, his eyes were drawn to that part of Melissa's anatomy. After enjoying the delicious curves beneath her blouse, he lifted his gaze and it slammed into hers. "Uh, I mean—"

"No, I'm not...anymore." She picked Mandy up and turned to leave the room.

Russ hurried after her, all the while reminding himself not to notice the sweet sway of her hips or her shapely calves as she preceded him. She was a mother, not some woman on the prowl!

He reached the kitchen in time to see her open the refrigerator door. Over her shoulder, he noticed a number of bottles already prepared on the middle shelf.

She removed the lid and nipple on one and stuck it in the microwave, setting the timer, all the while balancing Mandy on her hip.

"Want me to hold Mandy while you...do whatever else you need to do?" he asked belatedly.

She turned to look at him but drew back as if he'd threatened the baby. "No. That's all I need to do."

Puzzled, he took a step closer. Did she want his help or didn't she? "I could hold her, anyway, just to get her used to me."

"I don't think—" she began, then something changed her mind. "I suppose it wouldn't hurt just for a minute." She handed her daughter to him, her gaze sharp, as if she was afraid he might drop her.

"Do I have to support her head? I heard babies need that all the time," he said, staring at Mandy, who seemed just as surprised as he was that everything was going so well.

"Not really. At seven months, she manages just fine, but—be careful."

He was so enthralled with the bundle of sweetness in his arms that he only vaguely noted her mother's lack of confidence in his abilities.

"Hey, little girl, how're you doing?" he asked softly, then panicked when the smile she'd had on her lips turned into a frown.

"What's wrong? Did I do something wrong?" he asked. His panic seemed to be conveyed to his charge, and she whimpered.

Immediately Melissa scooped her child back into her arms. "No. She isn't used to having a man hold her."

Russ was amazed at the loss he felt with Mandy's removal from his arms. With another part of his mind he was processing the information he'd just received from her mother.

"You don't date." It wasn't a question, because he already knew the answer. The real question was why not.

She shot him a guarded look. "No." The microwave dinged and she took the bottle out.

When he realized she had to screw on the lid and nipple, he held out his hands for the baby. "Let me try again."

"No, I can—"

"Come on, Melissa. I'm not going to drop her." He reached for Mandy, feeling more confident on his second try.

Melissa hurriedly fixed the bottle, then reached for Mandy, who wasn't upset this time.

"I could feed her," Russ said.

Somehow, he wasn't surprised by Melissa's rejection of his offer.

He was beginning to get the idea that while Melissa might want to sleep in, she wasn't comfortable with strangers handling her child. "Do you take her to those church programs where they keep the baby for a few hours every week?"

"Mother's Day Out? No. Those places spread germs. Mandy's never sick because Mrs. Tuttle and I are the only ones who take care of her."

"Who is Mrs. Tuttle?"

"She's a neighbor. She says she's Mandy's granny, since she doesn't have one. She keeps Mandy while I go to work."

"You couldn't get her to give you a morning to sleep in?" he asked.

"Not really. Mrs. Tuttle tires easily. I wouldn't ask her to keep Mandy overnight. It's enough that she looks after her from noon to four. I bring the rest of my work home and do it after Mandy goes to bed."

"Sounds like you're a very busy lady." He noted the shadows under her eyes, but she had been remarkably cheerful since he'd arrived.

"Yes, but Mandy is worth everything. You probably don't think that since I'm asking for a break. But it's just for one morning. As a Mother's Day present. I thought—I'll understand if you want to take a pass," she said abruptly.

"So what baby-sitters do you use when you go out at night?" he asked, ignoring her offer. "If you have a good one, we could have one evening out this weekend, my treat. After all—"

"No. I don't leave Mandy at night."

Uh-huh. "What about Lindsay? I bet she'd be glad to take care of Mandy Saturday evening."

Melissa left the kitchen. By the time Russ caught up with her, she was sitting in a corner of one of the couches, the nipple of the bottle already in Mandy's rosebud mouth.

He crossed the room to sit in the green leather chair again. "What about Lindsay?" he reminded her.

"She has too much going on right now."

"Don't tell me she's never offered to help you out. I know Lindsay better than that."

Melissa kept her gaze on Mandy's little face. "Of course she offered, in the beginning. But…but it was too hard to let anyone take over for me. Mandy is my responsibility, since Greg's not here."

"Greg was your fiancé?"

"Yes."

"So you think he'd want you to drive yourself batty taking care of your baby with almost no help?" He wasn't sure why he was pushing so hard on this issue. Maybe it was because it seemed a waste for a beautiful woman to cut herself off from the male population like this.

Or maybe it was because he wanted the opportunity to spend some time with her, without the baby.

He immediately rejected that idea. He had no interest in a mother of any age.

She stiffened and fired him a glare that almost singed his toes. "Russ, I am not batty just because I would like to sleep in one morning."

He almost smiled but knew that reaction would irritate her even more. And he had another question for her, one that he wanted answered, even if it was none of his business.

"And did you also promise Greg that you'd remain alone the rest of your life?"

CHAPTER THREE

MELISSA WAS STUNNED by his question. He had no business asking such personal questions. Since Greg's death, she hadn't had to explain herself to anyone, and she wasn't going to now. "I don't think that's any of your business."

He didn't say anything.

When she turned her back on him, however, he asked, "Why are you so upset over a simple question?"

"My private life is none of your business."

"You invited me into your personal life, Melissa. I had a pleasant, *impersonal* weekend planned, lots of glitz, glamour and activity. You're the one who altered it."

"Well, I've changed my mind. I don't want a *personal* weekend." Then she added grudgingly, "Even if you are good with Mandy."

"Thanks. I like her, too," he said with a grin that made him all the more attractive.

Mandy complained and Melissa realized she'd let the bottle slip out of the baby's mouth. "Sorry, sweetie," she whispered.

"Need me to take over? I'd pay attention."

She gave him an exasperated look. "No, I do not. Why don't you go to bed, or watch television. I don't need your help."

"I'm trying to learn about Mandy so I can let you sleep in."

"No! I told you I've changed my mind. It was a silly thought. If you want to fulfill your part of the bargain, you can model for me tomorrow." She looked away from his fit body, trying to avoid thinking about sketching him. Or photographing him.

"Model? Like at the auction?"

She swallowed, her throat suddenly dry, as she remembered Russ's strut across the stage, a sexy grin on his face. "No, but do you have the outfit you wore?"

"The cowboy stuff? Nope, but I've got a pair of jeans with me. And the swimsuit you asked for." He tilted his head, his blue-eyed gaze fixed on her. "What would I be modeling for?"

"I've got an idea for a new line of greeting cards. My clients are asking for cowboy-oriented cards for tourists. When I saw you at the auction, it occurred to me I could base my character on you."

"So I'd pose and you'd draw me?"

She nodded. It wasn't that she was as intent on her plan as she had been. She'd been too tired after Mandy's birth to even think of starting something new. But she was grateful that she'd distracted him from his earlier question.

"Nude?"

She dropped Mandy's bottle as she stared at him,

openmouthed. Mandy instantly sent up a loud protest.

"I think I'd better take over the feeding. It will be good practice for me and keep Mandy from getting upset." As he was talking, he got up from the leather chair and scooped the baby and her bottle out of Melissa's arms. By the time she pulled herself together, banishing the image of Russ posing nude, he and Mandy were enjoying themselves.

"I was—you shouldn't—of course not nude. I don't do those kind of cards!" Guiltily, she remembered her idea about him in a bathtub. But that wouldn't really be nude. No one would know what he wore below water level.

"I didn't think you did," he assured her soothingly, as if she were Mandy.

"Then why did you—you were trying to upset me!"

"Not exactly. But a little teasing never hurts anyone, does it? Laughter is good for everyone." His gaze dropped to her child. "Do we have to stop and burp her?"

"Not until she finishes the bottle."

"When she gets up in the morning, does she get a bottle?"

"Yes, but you don't have to worry about the morning. I'll get up with her. She's an early riser."

"So am I."

"I told you I'd changed my mind. Don't you ever listen?" she demanded, frustration overtaking good manners.

"Yes, ma'am," he said, still grinning. Then, as if he hadn't noted her anger, he said, "You know, feeding a baby is kind of soothing. If I did this every night, I might not be so stressed out in my job."

"Then maybe you should be asking *yourself* about dating, not me," she retorted, then closed her eyes in dismay. Why did she have to remind him of his earlier question?

As if he could read her mind, he smiled again.

"Don't you like your job?" she hurriedly asked.

"It's all right. The salary is more than I'd ever hoped to make, but the work is dull, uncreative. I'd like more variety. You can only do so much when you're designing office buildings."

"Do you ever design houses?"

He gave her a wry grin that was charming. "At home. Never on the job."

Before she could ask any more questions, he took the bottle from Mandy's mouth. "This little lady is finished. Now what? I burp her?"

"Yes. Put her on your shoulder and rub her back."

He carefully maneuvered the baby to the right position. Melissa appreciated the care he showed, but she wished he'd give Mandy back to her. She felt vulnerable without her baby in her arms.

In almost no time, a loud burp ripped out of Mandy and brought a chuckle to Russ. "This kid has a definite talent. Too bad she's a girl."

Melissa's hackles rose at once. Her fiancé's parents had expressed disappointment that she gave birth to a girl. They'd hoped for a replacement for their son. Fortunately, they lived in Colorado and she and Mandy seldom saw them. "What's wrong with girls?" she challenged.

"Nothing. But I don't think girls indulge in burping contests like boys. With her talent, Mandy could win every time."

Melissa relaxed, smiling. "Hopefully she won't join in those contests."

"Do we put her in bed now?"

"After another diaper change. I'll take her." She hoped he'd remain in the living room, giving her some breathing space. She wasn't used to having a man around the house.

But he didn't take the hint. He followed right behind her, standing at her elbow as she changed Mandy, then tucked her into her bed, winding the animal mobile over her crib that played a lullaby.

Once they'd tiptoed out of the baby's room and Melissa had closed the door behind them, she headed for the kitchen to make sure everything was cleaned up and ready for the morning.

Russ followed.

"I'm just straightening up. Feel free to watch television or—or I've got a couple of murder mysteries you might want to read."

"You trying to get rid of me?"

"Uh, no, of course not." Why would she want to get rid of a tall, handsome man, one who made her think about long, hot kisses and passion-filled nights? That involuntary thought appalled her.

"Good."

Russ grinned as Melissa turned around with a flounce and hurried to the kitchen. She was such an easy target for his teasing. He hadn't had this much fun in years.

Considering how his afternoon had started, with the baby on the airplane screaming for an hour and a half, things had greatly improved. If anyone had asked him if he'd willingly spend three days with an overprotective single mom and a seven-month-old baby girl, he'd have assured them they were crazy.

Yet, given the opportunity several times by Melissa to walk away, he'd refused. There was something about her, other than her trim, gently curved body, sparkling brown eyes and stubborn chin, that made him want to linger.

Of course, he felt he owed her since she'd paid for this weekend. And the money from the auction meant the boys ranch could continue to help other kids like him.

He had to give Melissa credit. She was taking care of her child, unlike his mother. Maybe that was why he wanted to give her a break. She was being a good mother, even when she was tired. Had his mother been exhausted? Too worn-out to go on?

"Russ?"

Her voice, warm and husky, lured him from his thoughts.

"Yeah?"

"Are you sure you don't want to go to a hotel?"

"Are you afraid to have me stay here, Melissa? I promise I won't take advantage of you."

"No, of course not!" she returned at once, her cheeks blazing. "I trust you not to—"

"Then quit worrying. We'll all get a good night's sleep and tomorrow we'll decide what to do."

Tenderness filled him as the worry eased on Melissa's face. He immediately frowned. What was going on? He wasn't a nurturer. He believed in survival of the fittest. But there was something about Melissa that got to him.

"You changed your mind?" she asked.

"No, why would you think that?"

"You frowned."

He grinned again and reached out to caress her cheek lightly. "I was thinking of something else."

She stepped away. "There are fresh towels in the bathroom. If you don't mind, I think I'll go on to bed. Mandy gets up early."

He refrained from reminding her again that he got up early, too. In fact, he loved the early hours, before the world got into high gear. She probably hoped he'd stay in the bedroom until noon, leaving her alone.

No such luck.

"Of course I don't mind. Sweet dreams."

She seemed startled by his words. He was, too. Lindsay's mother had always wished each of the boys the same thing each night—probably because she'd had to deal with too many nightmares.

But it had been a long time since he'd heard or voiced that wish himself.

RUSS SLOWLY CAME AWAKE at first light the next morning. Amazing how different the sunshine seemed to be in Wyoming compared to Chicago. Brighter, cleaner, more invigorating.

He'd slept amazingly well. Melissa's sheets were soft, faintly scented, inviting. And the quiet of the morning, punctuated by birds chirping and a breeze blowing, was a huge contrast to his apartment perched above the rushing traffic. He'd been in Chicago almost fourteen years, since high school.

Had he reached his limit? Was it time to come home? He had to admit the idea had crossed his mind a few times lately. If Melissa didn't have anything for him to do today, he'd look around, talk to friends, scout out some possibilities.

He swung back the cover and got out of bed, his mind excited by his thoughts. After dressing in a pair of running shorts and shoes, carrying a T-shirt in case he got cold, he prepared to slip out for a brisk morning jog. Then he heard Mandy stirring.

He immediately pictured Melissa's face as she'd spoken of sleeping in one morning. Why not three? He crossed the hall and entered the baby's room. Mandy was already standing in the bed, reaching for the animals dangling from the mobile above her crib, babbling softly as if they were pets.

"Hi, little girl," he whispered, approaching her slowly, hoping she remembered him.

"Da-da-da-da," she jabbered at him with a grin.

While he was relieved that she treated him as friend, not foe, he was stunned by her response.

"Lord have mercy, I'm not your daddy, little girl. I hope you don't know what you're saying."

He reached for a disposable diaper and laid her down in the bed. "Let's see if I can do as good a job as Mommy. Eeew, you're a little stinky this morning." He dumped the nighttime diaper in the diaper pail and hastily replaced it with a fresh one. Her sleeper was also wet and he stripped it from her.

He and Mandy stared at each other. "What do you wear?" he asked, as if she could tell him. There was no response, of course, other than nonsensical syllables. He turned to the small white chest of drawers. After a brief search he found a pink, long-sleeved shirt and matching knit bottoms and decided Mandy could wear those clothes until her mother decided differently.

Next they adjourned to the kitchen. Carefully preparing a bottle as Melissa had last night, Russ settled on the couch and fed Mandy. He immediately noted one difference from the previous night. Mandy ran her tiny hand through his chest hair and then clamped down on a thick tuft.

"Hey, Mandy, that's not a handle," he muttered, and removed the bottle to pry her fingers loose. She offered a complaint that he feared would wake Melissa. He returned the bottle to her mouth at once, and she promptly resumed her hold on him.

"Okay. I guess I lost that debate," he acknowledged with a wry grin. He supposed her clutching his chest hair didn't matter. As long as she didn't try to remove any.

Once the bottle, and the impressive burp, had been completed, Russ wasn't sure what to do. He'd intended to jog and regretted not being able to. When his gaze passed over a navy-blue object near the coat closet, it took several seconds for him to register what he'd discovered.

An umbrella stroller.

"Hey, is Mom a jogger?" he asked Mandy.

She gurgled and tried to pull herself up to a standing position.

"Whoa! Let me help you before I have a bare patch on my chest," he hastily offered.

Rising from the couch, Mandy in his arms, he crossed the room and opened the stroller. He'd seen a lot of women, and men, too, jogging while pushing their children in strollers like this.

"Want to go for a run, Mandy? Would you be good?"

Mandy clapped her hands together and beamed at him.

Well, he'd said something she liked. He lowered her into the stroller and fastened the safety belt across her little tummy. She seemed secure, so he stepped back down the hall and softly pushed opened the office door.

Melissa was sound asleep on the sofa, wrapped in a blanket that had worked loose from one leg, exposing a well-muscled calf that he had a sudden urge to stroke. Quickly, he closed the door.

Jogging would knock those thoughts out of his mind, he hoped. A lot of jogging.

Mandy seemed to be trying to get out of the stroller when he got back to the living room. "Mandy, what are you doing? Are you ready to go?"

Again she clapped her hands.

He stared at her. "Go?"

She clapped.

"Well, I'll be darned. You know that word, don't you? I'm going to have to be careful what I say around you."

He hurried back down the hall to her room and found a baby blanket to tuck around her. It might be May, but that didn't mean early mornings in Wyoming would be warm.

After wrapping her up, he pulled the stroller to the front door and opened it quietly. After he and Mandy were outside, he pulled it to, leaving it unlocked. He didn't know where Melissa kept her keys, and he didn't want to be locked out.

"Mommy will be fine until we get back, right, Mandy? At least she's getting to sleep in. She'll thank us when we return."

In fact, he was filled with a sense of satisfaction. Already he could give Melissa what she appeared to so desperately need—a break from mothering.

Along with his satisfaction at being back in Wyoming and the pleasure of physical exercise, this morning was turning out to be very special.

"Here we go, Mandy. Hang on!"

The unlikely pair jogged up the street.

Melissa's house was on the western edge of town. The Platte River cut through the area not too far away. Ridges and plateaus backed up behind the neighborhood and he could catch sight of higher mountains in the distance.

He drew a deep breath of fresh air and relaxed. He was home. Maybe to stay.

MELISSA TURNED OVER...and almost fell off her abbreviated bed. She caught herself and flopped back onto her pillow, settling the blanket over the leg that was exposed.

Nice. She loved waking up without the alarm clock jolting her from unconsciousness. Her eyes drifted down. She'd try to sleep until it went off, though. She needed every minute she could get. Mandy would be up soon.

The next time she opened her eyes, she knew she had indeed fallen back asleep again. She felt too good. As she stretched, her feet hit the end of the couch. She reached over for the alarm clock, then remembered she'd promised herself she'd stay in bed until Mandy woke her this morning.

Checking her wristwatch, she noted the time—7:47. She slipped her arm under the blanket again. Then reality hit her. Why hadn't Mandy awakened her?

She scrambled from the couch and reached for the robe she'd left handy. After all, she had a guest. A very sexy guest. Tying the belt on her robe, she hurried to Mandy's room.

Her eyes rounded in shock as she discovered the

empty crib. Whirling around, she raced to the kitchen. No one was there.

Running back down the hall, she threw open Russ's bedroom door. Empty.

She checked the bathroom, then retraced her steps, revisiting each room of the house again. Blind panic built at an incredible speed until she couldn't think.

All she knew was that her baby was gone.

She ran around the house like a crazy woman until she forced herself to take a deep breath and think logically. He wouldn't take her baby. He didn't even know anything about babies. He'd been gentle with Mandy.

So where were they?

She checked the house once more, then opened the front door and stepped outside, scanning the neighborhood, looking for one bachelor and her beloved little girl.

RUSS WENT FOR A LONG JOG, alternating a brisk walk with his running. The rise as the road climbed to a ridge was more of a challenge than the gym in Chicago. And more fun, too. Invigorating exercise, coupled with clean air, was a great way to start his day. And Mandy, snug in her stroller beneath the blanket, had fallen back asleep, seemingly content with their agenda.

Even more important, Melissa had gotten some extra sleep. He couldn't keep his mind from his hostess. She was an attractive woman, but even more so because of her dedication to her child.

Not that he was interested, of course. He'd decided long ago he wasn't going to marry and have a family. It was too risky.

He was content living alone, being responsible only for himself.

Look what had happened to Melissa.

His gaze fell on the sleeping child. How would Melissa feel if given the chance to have a life without Mandy? Instinctively, he knew she'd never give up her child, no matter what hardships presented themselves.

Unlike his mother.

Of course, Melissa had several advantages over his mother. She was older, an adult. She had an education and an income that meant she didn't have to worry about her child starving.

When he'd first come to the ranch, Lindsay's mother told him he'd been thin as a rail. It had taken several months of hearty cooking to put any meat on his bones. And a lot of encouragement to get him to eat. She said she thought he'd been mourning his mother's disappearance.

He no longer cared about the woman, he assured himself, frowning fiercely.

He turned the corner of Melissa's street, slowing to a walk again. He'd taken several steps toward the house before he saw Melissa standing on the porch, looking up and down the street. He knew immediately what was wrong when she saw him. She practically collapsed against the side of the house.

"Damn!" he muttered. He hadn't thought about

how worried she would be. He'd assumed she would figure out where they were...if she woke up. With luck, he'd hoped she would sleep the entire time they were gone.

So much for a cooldown. He picked up the pace again, anxious to reassure Melissa that her baby was safe.

CHAPTER FOUR

"HOW DARE YOU!" Melissa yelled as Russ rolled the stroller up to her. She immediately knelt on the grass to unstrap Mandy.

"How dare I what?" he demanded, breathing heavily.

"Take my baby without telling me," she snapped, cuddling Melissa against her shoulder, running her hands all over the baby, as if checking her for an injury.

Russ stared at her, irritation replacing concern. He'd only been trying to help.

"Melissa, dear, are you all right?" a gentle soprano voice called from the porch next door.

Melissa still knelt on the grass clutching Mandy to her. Mandy, who was awake now, began to fret.

Russ bent forward to help Melissa up, despite his growing impatience, but Melissa drew back as if he'd attacked her. That brought the old lady on the porch rushing over.

Russ glared at Melissa. "Could you tell me what I've done? I was trying to help you, not hurt you. And I only did what you asked me to do."

She gave him a blank look, as if he'd spoken a

foreign language. "I asked you to take Mandy without permission?"

"He took Mandy?" the old lady asked with a gasp, reaching out to the baby as if she needed to touch her to be sure she was safe. "You want me to call the police?"

Russ rolled his eyes in exasperation. He was wearing athletic shoes, nylon jogging shorts and nothing else. He'd had a T-shirt on, but he'd taken it off partway through his run and put it around his neck. He didn't think he looked like a criminal, but Melissa's neighbor apparently didn't share his opinion.

"Oh, Mrs. Tuttle, no!" Melissa exclaimed, affording Russ some relief. "It was a misunderstanding."

But his dander was up now. "No, it wasn't. You said you wanted to sleep late. So, you slept late. I did what you asked me to do." How many times did he have to say it?

"One morning! I asked for one morning!" she exclaimed in return.

"So, you're getting better value for your money." He leaned closer and touched Mandy's cheek. "Mandy and I are a good team, aren't we, baby?"

"Well, that's certainly a change of attitude from last night," Melissa grumbled. "You didn't know which end was up then."

"He spent the night with you?" Mrs. Tuttle asked, shock on her face.

Melissa sent him a look that said, *This is all your fault.*

He couldn't hold back a grin. It wasn't often, he'd

guess, that Melissa was accused of being a scarlet lady. And all because she wanted to sleep late. Alone.

"Uh, yes, he— It's not what you think," Melissa assured her neighbor. "He's going to do some modeling—"

"He's a model?" the lady asked, running her gaze over his body.

Russ hadn't been so thoroughly checked out in a long time. He smiled at Mrs. Tuttle, but he felt his cheeks heating up.

"No!" Melissa protested. "He's not—this is ridiculous."

If it had been left up to Russ, he might have suggested that her neighbor mind her own business and ignored the questions. But Melissa had to live in the neighborhood. She wouldn't want her neighbors thinking she was a—he grinned at the thought— loose woman.

"Look, why don't we go inside," he suggested. "I'm dying for a cup of coffee. Maybe Mrs. Tuttle could join us and we could clear up all the confusion."

Melissa's look of gratitude was a big improvement over the accusing glares she'd been sending him. She turned to Mrs. Tuttle. "Come on in, won't you? This is all a little bizarre, but perfectly innocent. Russ was trying to help, even if he did go about it the wrong way."

"Hey!" he protested again, but both ladies were already on their way to the front door, completely ignoring him. With a shrug of his shoulders, he hurried after them.

Once they were inside, Mrs. Tuttle reached out for Mandy. "I'll change the little dear and give her her breakfast while you put on coffee," she said to Melissa.

Russ cleared his throat. "Look, I didn't mean to alarm you. I really thought I was doing something that would make you happy."

"I know," Melissa confessed with a sigh. "You're the last person anyone would suspect of kidnapping a baby. You don't even like them."

Twenty-four hours earlier, Russ would have been in complete agreement with that statement. It surprised him at the protest that rose up in him today. But he didn't say anything.

"I panicked," Melissa explained. "Mandy and I—we do everything together. I didn't know what had happened." She sighed. "I suppose I should confess that I'm not at the top of my game when I first wake up."

The thought of Melissa, all rumpled and warm, in the middle of a big bed was so enticing it took him a minute to respond. "Uh, yeah. You said you weren't a morning person."

Those big brown eyes of hers blinked several times, and he caught himself leaning closer, his gaze dropping to her lips, her rosy, kissable lips.

"Um, I'll go put on a pot of coffee. Would you like some breakfast, too?"

Breakfast? His head was spinning with thoughts of

tasting her, not food. And his body was rapidly responding in ways he couldn't control...or hide, since he was wearing those thin jogging shorts. "Uh, yeah, great. I'll go catch a shower," he added, backing away. A cold shower.

MELISSA HEADED for the kitchen, taking a deep breath. What had just happened? She didn't want to put a name to it, but if she did, it would be sexual attraction.

Why? She'd been around attractive men before. Maybe no one quite as handsome as Russ, but in the end, looks didn't matter all that much. So why was this man so dangerous to her peace of mind?

His smile certainly rated him at the top of her list of sexy men. It enticed her to smile back, to share his amusement. To enjoy life.

His caring for Mandy was another point in his favor. A big point. Even though he'd arrived knowing nothing about babies, he hadn't hesitated to bond with her baby daughter. So much so that Mandy had been perfectly happy with him this morning.

But her body wasn't responding to his solicitousness over Mandy. Her body was revving up its engine every time he drew near. So much so that she feared losing control. That hadn't happened in a long time.

Mrs. Tuttle came out of Mandy's room. "This little lady is ready for breakfast. Shall I make her cereal?"

Melissa managed a smile. "Of course."

Before she could turn away, she saw Mrs. Tuttle look around her as if searching for something. Then she asked, "Where is that man?"

Melissa shrugged her shoulders. The answer wasn't going to reassure her neighbor. "He's taking a shower. He'll join us in a few minutes."

The routine of preparing breakfast soothed Melissa's jangled nerves. Normally she grabbed a bowl of cereal or a piece of toast to start the day, but she couldn't offer that to Russ.

When the coffee had perked, she poured Mrs. Tuttle a cup, then one for both herself and Russ and carried them to the table, along with some bakery cinnamon rolls she'd warmed in the oven. "Help yourself, Mrs. Tuttle. I'll wait and scramble the eggs when Russ gets out of the shower." She scooped Mandy up from her high chair, then sat down to give the baby her bottle.

"Such a sweet child," Mrs. Tuttle said before she took a bite of cinnamon roll.

"Yes," Melissa agreed, grateful for the small talk. She wasn't anxious to start the explanations. What had seemed to her a simple arrangement had suddenly become complicated. And she didn't want Mrs. Tuttle to think she was behaving irresponsibly.

"You know, dear," Mrs. Tuttle began, her gaze fastened on the cinnamon roll in her hand, "there are a lot of diseases out there these days. You are being careful, aren't you?"

Melissa thought she would die of embarrassment.

"Mrs. Tuttle, really, there's no need—I mean, if I were—I know about the diseases, but I'm not."

"Oh."

"You sound disappointed," she exclaimed, thinking she must be mistaken.

Mrs. Tuttle's faded blue eyes twinkled. "Well, you've been alone for a while now. And a little excitement wouldn't go amiss, would it?"

"Mrs. Tuttle!" Melissa said, staring at the sedate little lady she'd lived next to for a long time.

Russ stepped into the kitchen, dressed in jeans, a knit shirt and running shoes. "Has Mrs. Tuttle done something she shouldn't?" he asked with a teasing grin.

The older woman smiled at him. "No, but I was hoping you had."

Melissa wanted to hide her face. Instead, she jumped to her feet and thrust her baby back at her neighbor. "Will you hold Mandy while I scramble the eggs?"

She abandoned the others while she cooked, keeping her back to them, but she couldn't shut out their conversation.

Russ introduced himself, adding, "I think I'm going to like you, Mrs. Tuttle."

Melissa knew Mrs. Tuttle was thrilled with Russ. It was in her voice as she asked him a dozen questions about why he was there. His patience amazed Melissa.

When she came to the table with freshly scrambled eggs and bacon, the two were getting along famously. "So now you know nothing was going on?" Melissa asked.

"Unfortunately, yes," her neighbor said with a sigh. "But I don't understand why you didn't ask me to keep Mandy so you could sleep late. You know I would be happy to do so."

"Oh, Mrs. Tuttle, you already do so much for me. I was afraid it would tire you out. Besides, I'd already paid for Russ's services." She sighed. "It was a crazy idea, and it went too far before I realized it. Anyway, I'm going to ask Russ to do some modeling for me and let that be the end of it."

Melissa noted that the other two exchanged a look, as if they had a conspiracy between them. But that couldn't be possible. They'd only just met, and Melissa had been present the entire time.

Russ offered her the plate of eggs and bacon he'd dished out.

"Uh, no, thank you," she responded, setting it down on the table.

"Now, dear, you need to eat something. I know you haven't had breakfast yet." Mrs. Tuttle nudged the plate closer to Melissa.

"I'm not very hungry."

"We don't want you to faint from lack of food," Russ said with a smile. "If you did, we'd have to call an ambulance and I think this neighborhood has had enough excitement for one morning."

Which reminded her of something she had to say. "I'm sorry I accused you of—of not doing the right thing. I realize you were only trying to help."

He grinned, seemingly pleased with her words. "I guess I don't know enough about mothers or I would've realized you'd be worried if you woke up and found Mandy gone."

Relieved that he was handling this so well, Melissa relaxed a little. "Well, at least it's all over. I'll take you to a hotel and—"

He interrupted her, smiling at Mrs. Tuttle. "She keeps trying to get rid of me. Look, Melissa, you paid for my company for the whole weekend—Friday to Sunday. You're going to get what you paid for."

"Russ, I'll be delighted for you to model for me. That will help me a lot. But I was wrong to include Mandy in my plans."

"Well, I'm not willing to repack. I hate packing, and I've already taken everything out of my suitcase. So I guess I'll have to stay."

She wasn't falling for that ridiculous line. "You only had a small suitcase. Don't make it sound like you packed for a month on the *Queen Mary*."

He turned back to the woman Melissa was beginning to think was his staunchest ally. "See? She keeps trying to get rid of me."

"I don't understand it," Mrs. Tuttle said, her eyes twinkling again. "A fine-looking man like you doesn't come along all that often."

"Mrs. Tuttle!" Melissa protested.

Russ just grinned, as if he'd won a prize.

"Maybe you should go back to Chicago, instead, and forget about modeling for me." She realized she was cutting off her nose to spite her face; she really wanted to do some cards based on Russ. But she had her sanity to think of.

"Oh, no, I can't leave without seeing my friends. I haven't even talked to Lindsay."

"I think she's out of town." Melissa kept her fingers crossed under the table. Lindsay had talked about being away for the weekend. Melissa hoped she was right.

He acted as if she hadn't spoken. Looking at Mrs. Tuttle, he said, "Did I tell you I'm thinking about moving back to Wyoming?"

"Now, that's good news!" the older woman responded.

"It is?" Melissa asked, surprised. "Why would you—"

"Because I don't want you and Mandy to move to Chicago," Mrs. Tuttle replied.

Melissa had thought she might die of embarrassment earlier, now she was sure of it. "Mrs. Tuttle, Mandy and I are not moving to Chicago. Can I get you some more coffee?" Maybe Russ wouldn't realize what her neighbor was implying by her crazy response if Melissa didn't say anything.

"I'll get it, dear. Eat some eggs now. What are you going to do today to entertain Russ?"

Melissa shook her head. "Entertain him? I thought I'd offer one last time to take him to a hotel or the airport, whichever he'd prefer. Then…I don't know."

Russ took another bite of eggs, then smiled at her.

"I'm not going to a hotel. The food wouldn't be nearly as good as yours. I'm a sucker for a home-cooked meal."

"You're being ridiculous."

"No, I'm not. Hotel food is so unappetizing."

"That's true," Mrs. Tuttle chimed in. "Once I stayed at a motel in Denver and the coffee shop there burned my eggs. Oh, it was terrible. Of course, they offered to fix me some more, but what would be the point? I mean, they'd probably be burned, too."

Melissa covered her eyes with one hand. She would never do anything to hurt Mrs. Tuttle's feelings, but she suspected her friend was deliberately trying to keep Russ right where he was.

"See?" Russ said, a grin on his face.

The man was actually smiling.

"How can you sound so cheerful? I accused you of snatching my baby!"

Mrs. Tuttle chuckled. "Think what a great story it will make to tell your grandchildren. I bet the other kids won't have a good story like that about how their grandparents met."

Melissa's eyes almost popped out of her head as she stared at the sweet little lady from next door. "Mrs. Tuttle! What are you talking about? We're not—I mean, Russ is not—"

Even Russ's sangfroid had disappeared. "We're not dating, you know. I'm just here for the weekend. Then I go back to Chicago."

"Oh, of course, silly me. I don't know what I was

thinking of. Do you like Chicago better than Wyoming?"

Russ shrugged. "I've liked it all right, but as I said, I'm thinking of moving back. So I guess I have to say I prefer Wyoming."

Mrs. Tuttle smiled at him. "Do you have family in the area?"

Russ filled her in on his background at the boys ranch. Normally he didn't talk about it to anyone, much less a stranger. But then, he could hardly count the motherly Mrs. Tuttle a stranger anymore.

"Oh, you poor thing," she cooed.

"I made it," he muttered, looking away from the two women. The last thing he wanted was pity, especially Melissa's.

"Oh my, yes. And I expect your mother knew you'd be better off there. That's so hard on a young girl, especially back then. The world was cruel to single mothers."

Lindsay's mother had expressed the same sentiment once, but Russ hadn't been willing to listen. Now Mrs. Tuttle's words struck him hard.

"Mrs. Tuttle," Melissa interrupted, "would you like some orange juice?"

Had she realized how much Mrs. Tuttle's words had affected him? Russ wondered. He was amazed at how intuitive she seemed to be to his feelings. It had never happened with a woman before.

What was going on with him?

"Why, no, dear, I believe not," Mrs. Tuttle said.

"I'd better get back home. I haven't fed my kitty yet, what with all the excitement."

"Thank you for helping with Mandy this morning," Melissa said softly.

"You know I love her," Mrs. Tuttle assured her. Russ could see there was a real bond between the two women. They hugged, then Melissa headed toward the front door.

As the elderly lady walked by Russ's chair, she patted him on the shoulder. "You're a nice young man. Welcome to the neighborhood."

"Thank you, Mrs. Tuttle," he said, standing.

She paused and looked him up and down. "Oh my, yes. You two will make wonderful babies."

Then she walked out of the house, leaving Melissa and Russ gaping at each other.

[...]

[...]

CHAPTER FIVE

THE SOUND OF THE DOOR closing behind Mrs. Tuttle
signaled a release of the tension. Both Melissa and
Russ burst into laughter simultaneously.

Melissa collapsed into her chair, holding her sides,
and Russ joined her at the table, warm chuckles filling the room.

Finally, wiping away the tears that had escaped her
eyes, she said, "I promise I'll explain to her...again.
She's really not as dotty as she seemed."

"It's okay. What she thinks won't hurt me."

Melissa sobered. "I'm really sorry about what
happened earlier. I accused you of—"

He shrugged and grinned. "Get over it, Melissa.
You got upset because you care about your child."

Sighing, she leaned back in her chair. "I still think
you should cut your losses and head back to Chicago."

"Nope, the subject is closed. I'm staying right
here. Besides, I'm learning a lot."

She hesitated to ask for clarification, but she
couldn't help herself. "About what?"

"Babies," he responded promptly. "As you
pointed out, I didn't know anything about taking care

of a baby until I got here." He took a sip of coffee and grinned at her. "When I go home, I'll probably pick up some extra money baby-sitting on the weekends."

"Yeah, right," she returned, not believing him for a minute.

Then he surprised her, his face turning serious. "I'm not sure I want to—or can—explain, but I need to stay. I'm working through something, and being around Mandy will help me. I think I've got to deal with my past so I can—can prepare for the future."

She knew he must be talking about his childhood at the ranch and maybe the years before. He hadn't mentioned much about his mother, though he must have some memory of her since he was four when she left him. And, darn it, after what he'd said, she couldn't ask any questions!

"I'll do anything I can to help you, but didn't Mrs. Tuttle's implications send panic through your veins? You're a career bachelor if I ever saw one. Aren't you afraid I'm trying to trap you?"

He grinned. "As many times as you've tried to shove me out the door? I don't think so."

"Reverse psychology?" she offered with a grin.

"Too risky," he assured her. "I might take you up on it."

With an exasperated look, she repeated his words. "I don't think so. You're too stubborn."

He gave her a superior look. "It takes one to know one."

Even as she shook her head, she started to laugh.

And wondered again how she was going to keep this man at a distance. She had to accept his decision to stay in her house. After all, it had been her idea in the first place. But life would be easier if she could put some distance between them. She didn't like the response her body, or her emotions, had to this man.

He stared at her. "I'm only going to be here until Sunday. You can stand me that long, can't you?"

She nodded, trying to hide her unease.

"Good. Now, tell me what you had in mind for your company. By the way, I don't even know what kind of pictures you want to use. Cowboy shots, you said?"

Next to Mandy, her company was her pride and joy. With good reason. She'd created both of them. "My company's name is Wyoming Bright. A lot of my customers are tourists, and when I saw you on the stage, I thought a cowboy would be perfect for my cards."

"Makes sense. So, do I pose like a statue?"

Melissa swallowed at the immediate vision of Russ posing for her. In her art school days, she'd drawn men in the nude with no reaction. But her mouth suddenly went dry at the thought of Russ—no, she'd better not go there.

"Um, actually, I wanted to take some pictures of you. Sometimes I use photos on my cards. Even if I wanted to sketch, I could do it from the photos."

"That sounds easy enough."

"But you don't have to do this! I release you from your promise. In fact, I insist that we're even. Maybe not even. I probably owe you. That's why I'm willing to pay—"

Russ ignored her. "What should I wear?"

Before she could try again, he stood and carried his dishes to the sink.

"But—"

"I have jeans and a plaid shirt. And boots. If we went out to the ranch, I could borrow a Stetson, maybe a belt buckle."

"That's fine, but—"

"Why did I need to bring a swimsuit?"

Now she really was embarrassed. "Oh, no reason. It was a stupid idea and—and I think you've suffered enough from my stupid ideas."

He let that comment slide by and went off on another tangent. "What about Mandy? Will she come with us or stay with Mrs. Tuttle?"

Melissa was getting frustrated with herself for being so dithery. She had a job to do and she would do it. She stood. "I'll take Melissa with us. You'll need to be ready in half an hour." She raised her chin and stared at him. "And bring your swimsuit."

He grinned again. "I suspected there was a take-charge lady in there somewhere. Otherwise you wouldn't have survived everything you've been through. Way to go!"

His approval pleased her more than she would have thought. It had been a long time since anyone had praised her. She swallowed again. "Thank you, and you have twenty-nine minutes left."

He reached out and cupped one cheek, surprising

her. The warmth of his touch almost undermined her determination. Almost. She stepped back, dislodging his hand.

"Don't be so skittish," he said, but he withdrew his hand, tucking it in his back pocket. "I don't need that much time. Mandy seems content in her high chair for now, so go get dressed. I'll watch her. After all, I'm not the one still dressed for bed."

She stared down at herself, having completely forgotten she was still clothed in her ratty bathrobe and nightgown. What a morning! "Oh, of course, I—can you manage?"

He seemed offended by her doubt. "Of course I can. Though, as I've already told you, she's the first baby I've ever been around. My friends don't have babies."

"None of them?" she asked incredulously.

He grimaced. "One or two have married and have children, but I usually don't see them once they make those changes in their lives."

"You just cut them out? Why?"

"Because they have other priorities, and we just don't have that much in common anymore. Now, go get dressed. Mandy and I will manage. Shoo!"

He leaned toward her, as if to kiss her, and Melissa scurried from the room. She'd trust him with Mandy, but not with herself.

As she dressed, her mind drifted to their conversation.

What was wrong with the man? She'd offered him a way out. Again and again. She'd embarrassed him, almost had him arrested. Her neighbor had tried to imply they would have babies together. He had to be insane to hang around after such treatment.

What did he mean about needing to stay? She didn't see how a weekend spent with her and Mandy would do anything for him. She was the one who'd planned to benefit by sleeping late, not him.

She recalled the look on his face when he said he needed to stay. Even if she didn't know what he meant, he'd been sincere. At least she thought so. Maybe she should just accept that, for whatever reasons, Russ wanted to spend the weekend with her and Mandy. The least she could do was make sure everything went smoothly.

THINGS WEREN'T GOING SMOOTHLY.

A call to the ranch revealed that Lindsay was indeed in Denver, visiting a friend, as Melissa had thought. So Russ wouldn't get a chance to visit with her.

He didn't seem upset by that turn of events, but Melissa was for his sake. Sam Duncan, Lindsay's uncle, had given them permission to come out and take photos, so they were on their way to the ranch, but Melissa was uneasy.

Mandy was in her car seat, of course, behind Russ. Next to her was the photography equipment, all the paraphernalia for a baby, and a picnic lunch.

"I think we should've leased a four-wheel-drive vehicle," Russ muttered as they jolted over the unpaved road toward Lightning Creek, the nearest town to the ranch.

"My car may not look like much, but it's very reliable," she assured him.

As if she'd uttered a curse with those words, a loud pop startled her and almost threw the car off the road. "What was that?" she said in panic as she struggled to keep the car on the gravel road.

"Sounds like a blowout to me."

As soon as she stopped, Russ opened his door and stepped out. "Yeah, right front tire is a goner. You do have a spare, don't you?"

Of course she had a spare. Didn't she? She'd never had a blowout before. She'd never changed a tire. Squaring her shoulders, she got out of the car. She'd figure it out. She had to.

"Of course. If you'll, um, get Mandy and—and stand to one side, I'll—" Do what? She usually didn't drive out of Casper, but she was a member of an auto club. Would they come out here to change her tire?

Unfortunately she didn't have a phone. They'd have to walk to the ranch and call the auto club from there. With a groan, she stared down the road. How much farther did they have to go?

"I have a better idea. *You* get Mandy and I'll take care of the tire change."

"No! It's my responsibility."

"Have you ever changed a tire before?" he asked.

She didn't answer that question. "The instructions are quite clear. I'm sure—"

"I guess not," he said dryly. He caught her by the shoulders. "I've changed a million of them. In college the car I had made yours look like a Mercedes. The tires were threadbare and didn't last long."

"How horrible! You could've been hurt or—"

He grinned again, that charming, devil-may-care grin that did strange things to her. "Yeah, but I survived. Now, step aside and watch my expertise." He took the keys from her hand and went to the trunk of the car. "Get Mandy out, just in case the car slips off the jack."

She hurriedly collected the baby, then followed him to the back of the car. "If we want to walk to the ranch, I can call the auto club I belong to."

"That would take too long. Besides, I'm wearing cowboy boots, not jogging shoes. They're not made for long walks."

He hefted the small spare tire out of the trunk, along with her jack and tire tool. He did seem to know what he was doing, so Melissa stood back and watched him work. It was a strange experience, letting someone else carry the load.

"You're supposed to be admiring my expertise, my muscles," Russ pointed out as he jacked up the car.

"I am," she hurriedly said. "I apologize for your having to do this. I should've—"

"It's not your fault. Your tires are in good shape. You must've hit something sharp."

He'd already loosened the lug nuts. After he'd gotten the car up high enough, he took the flat tire off and slid the smaller-size replacement tire in its place. He would see about getting the tire fixed tomorrow. Five minutes later, they were ready to go.

"Got anything I can wipe my hands on? I'd hate to mess up the inside of your car."

"Yes, of course." She strapped Mandy into her car seat again and reached for her purse. Pulling out a bottle, she handed it to Russ. "This is a dry wash."

He frowned. "A dry wash?"

"Yes, it'll clean your hands without water. It might not do a perfect job, but it will help."

"Very clever, Melissa. I've never used this stuff before."

She smiled. "With a baby, you have to be prepared for everything. Sometimes Mandy isn't as, um, sweet-smelling as she is right now."

Russ chuckled and held up a hand. "I don't want to know. But I can tell you horses aren't much better. I could've used some of this when I had to clean out the stables."

She was being seduced by his sense of humor.

That thought shocked her and she hurried around the car to the driver's side. "Ready?" she asked as he slid in, keeping her gaze on the road.

"Yeah. Are you all right?"

"Yes, of course. Why do you ask?"

"You seem upset. Did I do something wrong?"

"No, not at all." Nothing that she couldn't handle. She needed to concentrate on business. After all, that had been the first idea for buying a bachelor. Best not to forget it.

UNCLE SAM, AS RUSS called him, was very helpful. Russ had given the old man a hug, greeting him warmly. Sam had been a confidant for many of the boys. Though semiretired now, he was still a much-loved presence at Lost Springs.

He loaned Russ his almost-new Stetson and a belt buckle he'd won at a local rodeo when he was a boy. "Now you look like a cowboy."

Melissa seemed to agree. She nodded, smiling at him. "Sam's right. That's exactly the look I was hoping for."

"Okay. What now?"

"Can we go to the barn? I think I'd like to pose you sitting on a bale of hay. Or maybe with a horse. I'll get some ideas as we go along."

"What about Mandy?" he asked.

Melissa was holding her daughter while Russ gathered the essentials. "I have a frame that allows me to carry her on my back, like a papoose."

Sam stepped forward. "Well, now, I reckon I could carry the little girl. I'm not doing anything today."

"Good idea, Uncle Sam," Russ agreed without consulting Melissa. He lifted the baby out of her arms and passed her over to Sam.

Melissa started to protest, but she wasn't sure why. She'd take the frame with them. Sam might have to leave them after a while. A model shoot took a long time.

She gathered all her equipment, but Russ lifted it out of her hands. "I can carry it," she protested.

"You can, but why should you when I'm here? Except your camera, of course," he added, nodding at the one in her hands. "I don't want to mess up anything." He started off in the direction of the barn with her tripod, camera bag and baby frame. Sam followed with Mandy. When Melissa realized she was about to be left behind, she hurried after them.

For the next hour, she had Russ pose beside a stall where a quarter horse was kept. The curious animal nosed Russ as he stood there, leaning against the stall door, and he reached out to rub the horse's nose. Melissa caught it on film.

She had him sit on a bale of hay, one knee propped up and a blade of straw in his mouth. After several pictures, she asked him to tilt back the cowboy hat. She wanted to be sure his face could be clearly seen.

That face would sell a lot of cards.

As accommodating as he was, Melissa grew a little more daring. "Would you object to unbuttoning your shirt?"

His eyebrows rose. "Like at the auction?"

She nodded, her pulse speeding up.

"Sure, why not? Will it sell more cards?" he asked with a grin.

"Oh, yes," she muttered.

He laid the Stetson on the bale of hay, stood up and pulled his shirt out of his jeans. Then he began unbuttoning it.

A big grin on his face, Sam started humming a well-known strip song.

Melissa's cheeks flamed, but she began snapping

pictures. When Russ was halfway through unbuttoning, she called his name. He looked up, a grin on his face, and she took a picture that she knew would be perfect.

"I think you're enjoying this," she murmured.

"You bet, sweetheart. A man likes to be admired." His cocky grin fit the persona of a cowboy so well, Melissa wondered if he'd chosen the wrong profession.

"Are you sure you're an architect?"

His grin widened. "You bet. I can show you my sketches later."

She chuckled, his leering so blatant she knew he wasn't serious. But it made a great picture.

Suddenly, the atmosphere was disrupted by a cry from Mandy. Melissa had been so wrapped up in her work she'd almost forgotten she had her child with her. She let her camera hang by its strap and turned to Sam. "What's wrong?"

"I don't know. We were doin' just fine."

Melissa checked her watch. "Oh, she's probably hungry. It's past lunchtime." She turned to Russ. "We'll need to take a break."

"No problem. I wouldn't mind a little lunch myself."

"Of course. Why don't you and Sam share the picnic lunch while I feed Mandy." She'd already turned to head for the car when Russ stopped her.

"I'll feed Mandy and you can set out the food. Then we'll all eat. You're going to dry up and blow away if you don't start eating more."

His concern for her was both comforting and ir-ritating.

"I'm not a child, Russ."

"Nope, you're a beautiful woman juggling a lot of things. But I'm supposed to be helping you this weekend, not causing more problems."

He took Mandy from Uncle Sam and bounced her gently. "Hey, there, Mandy. Are you hungry? Let's go find some lunch for you." He and Sam turned and walked out of the barn.

Again Melissa hurried after them.

HALF AN HOUR LATER, Russ decided his plan had worked well. Mandy, fed and happy, lay on the blanket beside him, smiling as she played with a rattle Melissa had given her.

He, Sam and Melissa had enjoyed roast beef sandwiches made from last night's leftovers. They beat any he'd ever eaten. The lady could definitely cook.

She also seemed to know her way around a camera. He'd been impressed with her efficiency the past hour. He only hoped the results met her expectations.

"How long have you been a photographer?" he asked.

"My parents bought me my first camera when I was ten," she admitted. "I was fortunate that I could afford to experiment."

"So you taught yourself?"

"Mostly. I took some courses in photography when I was at art school."

"I bet some of them pictures will be real good,"

Sam commented. "If they're half as good as these sandwiches, I reckon you'll be rich."

"Thanks, Sam," Melissa said with a smile that lit up her face. "And you haven't even tasted my brownies yet."

"You brought brownies?" Sam asked, his smile eager.

In answer, she reached for a cookie tin and took the lid off, holding it out to the older man. He immediately took several brownies. Then she offered it to Russ.

He took one of the sweet squares and tasted it. "Mmm, I see what you mean. But I think I prefer the roast beef."

She smiled and said nothing.

"What do you have in mind for the rest of the afternoon?" he asked.

"If you're not too tired, I'd like some pictures of you on a horse. Would that be all right, Sam?"

"Sure. We got plenty of horses."

"You do know how to ride, don't you?" she asked Russ, a frown on her lovely face.

He grinned. "Sweetheart, not only can I ride a horse, I can saddle him, brush him, clean the tack and muck out the stall. We had to do everything."

"Hmm. Muck out the stalls?"

"Me and my big mouth," he muttered, but he was still grinning. He was enjoying being the focus of Melissa's attention.

"Would you take your shirt off to muck out the stalls?"

He groaned. "More beefcake shots? That doesn't go well with muck."

"Well, I don't think customers will mind since they can't smell it."

"Good point. Okay, sure, I'll do that." Then he remembered something else. "By the way, why did you want me to bring a swimsuit? Was that for more beefcake?"

Melissa's cheeks flamed as he waited for her answer.

CHAPTER SIX

"YOU THINKIN' OF GOING swimming?" Sam asked, frowning. "The water's still pretty cold in the river."

Melissa could feel Russ's curious stare. There was no way to ignore the question. "No, that's not what I had in mind. But I've changed my mind."

"Why?"

"Russ, really, haven't you had enough of my screwy ideas?" She gave him her best smile. "Let's get you on a horse. That will make some great pictures."

"I agree. But I'd still like to know what you had in mind."

She looked away from him. Even imagining what she'd wanted sent shivers through her body. Finally, she confessed. "A bubble bath."

Both men frowned.

Then Russ leaned closer. "Did I hear you right? A bubble bath? They're for girls."

She hurriedly explained. "You know that old, claw-footed bathtub on the porch of the ranch store? I thought a picture of you in a bubble bath, your hat still on your head, would—would make an amusing picture."

Russ stared at her, a frown on his face. "I don't mind unbuttoning my shirt, but taking a bath in public is going a little far."

"You're right, of course." She stood, both relieved that he'd rejected the idea and disappointed at the loss of a good photo opportunity.

Russ didn't move. "Why?"

"Why what?"

"Why me in a bathtub…with bubbles?"

Why wouldn't the wretched man drop the subject? She'd agreed that it wasn't a good idea. "Never mind."

"I want to know."

"Fine. It's the contrast. The big, sexy male doing something soft, sweet, feminine."

"Feminine?" he asked, outrage on his face.

It was almost laughable, his reaction, so typically male. She tried to explain it again. "It's like—like a picture of a big strong guy tenderly holding a baby. It's the unexpected gentleness that grabs a woman's heart."

His eyes narrowed in thought, but he said nothing.

"Never mind. We can forget about it."

He stood. "No. We'll do it. But I want some pictures of me and Mandy, too. Like you said."

Now it was her turn to frown. "Mandy? You want me to use Mandy as a model?"

"Why not? You're using *me*."

Melissa felt her hackles rise. "You're objecting? It seemed to me you were enjoying yourself, showing off."

"I was trying to be helpful, to give you your money's worth." He wasn't cracking that devil-may-care grin now.

Sam got to his feet, much slower than Russ, but he got there. "You want me to go empty that tub while you two finish this argument?"

"No!" Melissa snapped. She wouldn't ask Russ for the time of day after that remark.

"Yes!" Russ returned simultaneously.

Sam grinned and walked away. Melissa considered going after him, but she couldn't strong-arm the man, even if he was a lot older. Instead, she picked up Mandy and her camera and headed for her car.

Russ stopped her after two steps.

"Where are you going?"

"Home."

"What about the picture?"

"I think you've more than finished your servitude, Mr. Hall. I wouldn't want to take advantage of you." She kept her gaze on that muscular chest she'd been admiring half the day.

"Aw, hell, I didn't—come on, Melissa, you know I didn't mean it that way."

"Strange," she replied, her voice cool, "that's exactly how it sounded."

He muttered something under his breath, but she didn't ask for clarification. "If I grovel, will you forgive me?"

She tried to step around his large frame but he blocked her way. "Come on, Melissa, give me a break."

She gave him a brief smile that held no warmth. "It's quite all right. I don't want to take advantage of your generosity."

Without any warning, Russ bent his head and covered her lips with his. Shock held her immobile until Mandy gurgled. Then Melissa jumped back. She would have slapped him if she hadn't been holding Mandy and he hadn't grabbed her arm.

"How—how dare you!"

"Now, Melissa, that's a cliché, unless we've gone back in time a hundred years." He released her arm and chucked Mandy under the chin. "Right, Mandy? Tell Mom it was just a little kiss. Actually, you can consider it my taking advantage of you, which makes it okay for you to take advantage of me." He grinned as if waiting to be praised for his ingenuity.

She closed her eyes, unable to stop the trembling that seized her. Unable to breathe. No man had touched her since Greg died. No one had caressed her, held her, looked at her as a woman.

What bothered her most of all was the way her pulse had shot up, the way her lips had wanted to cling, the way she had betrayed Greg's memory.

Abruptly, she agreed. "Fine. I'll take advantage of you. Let's go make that picture." She whirled around to return to the picnic site, but Russ snatched Mandy from her arms before she could get away.

"I'll carry Mandy."

"Put her in the stroller I brought. It's in the back of the car." She walked off, hoping distance would calm her and that Russ wouldn't realize how shaken she was.

She gathered up what was left of the picnic and the blanket they'd sat on and followed him to the car. Russ had gotten the stroller out of the trunk and was settling Mandy in it.

Melissa stowed everything she carried in the trunk and trudged back to gather her equipment, not even looking at Russ.

Then she walked toward the ranch store, a few yards away. Sam was waiting on the porch steps. The amusement on his face told her he'd seen that ill-fated kiss, but she pretended she didn't notice.

"We're fillin' buckets with hot water, Melissa," Sam announced as soon as she got close. "You got some bubble stuff?"

"No, I didn't bring any. I—I wasn't sure we'd do the photo.

"But you told me to bring my swimsuit," Russ protested.

Several young boys from the ranch were standing nearby, watching their every move.

"I hadn't decided to do the shot for sure. But without bubbles, we certainly can't do it." She sent him a triumphant smile that hid her disappointment. There she went again, losing even as she won.

"I don't see why not. You just take the picture so my swimsuit doesn't show. Let's get this over with, so I can go get on a horse. It's been a few months since I've done any riding."

Melissa looked at him in surprise. And found her

gaze caught by his smile. He was enjoying himself? She'd thought he was irritated with her. She frowned.

He leaned closer, and she suddenly feared he intended to repeat that kiss. She reared back.

"The kids are watching," he warned. "We don't want them to think adults act like children, do we?"

Her startled gaze flew to the boys, who were studying them intently. She shook her head.

"Now," Russ said softly, "are you sure you don't have any of that bubble goop?"

She shook her head no. "That's why we should move on—"

"You want some bubbles?" one of the boys asked, stepping closer.

Russ ignored her attempt to turn the boy away. "Yeah. *You* got some bubble stuff?" His face wore a teasing grin.

The boy chuckled. "No, sir. But there's some in the store. You know, where you blow and it makes bubbles."

"Would that do?" Russ asked, and Melissa realized he was looking at her for an answer.

"Really, Russ, there's no need—"

"Do you ever answer questions?"

She felt her temper rising again. "Yes, I answer questions. And yes, the bubble stuff will work. And no, I'm not going to take your picture."

"Then I'm going to look like a damn fool sitting in a tub full of bubbles out in plain sight."

The two boys giggled.

"Watch your language in front of the children," she warned crisply.

There was that grin that sent her pulse racing. "Are you going to wash my mouth out with soap?"

His teasing made Melissa's mouth go dry and she tried to look away.

Fortunately for her, Russ walked over to the boys. "You fellows know where to get a couple of towels?"

"Sure!" one of them cried. Then his gaze went to Sam. "Is that okay?"

"You bet. Get'em out of my room." Then Sam turned around and went back into the store, and the kids took off for his cabin.

Suddenly, Russ and Melissa were alone on the porch, with only Mandy for a chaperone.

RUSS KNEW BETTER than to bring up the subject of the stolen kiss. But he wanted to. He wanted to pull her into his arms and repeat that kiss. But neither choice was acceptable.

And if he didn't do something quickly, she would probably warn him not to touch her again. He didn't want those words spoken, either.

"Watch Mandy, will you?" he said, stepping away from the stroller to sit down on the top step of the porch. The baby squealed as she saw him walk away from her, one little hand reaching out as if to catch him.

"What are you doing?" Melissa asked.

He looked over his shoulder to see her frowning.

"Nothing scandalous yet. I'm taking off my boots. I don't want to put them in the water, right? You just asked that I wear the hat."

"That's right. It would be absurd to wear boots in a bathtub."

"Right. But a hat makes sense." He said the words solemnly, but then he couldn't hold back a grin.

"The—the audience has to know you're a cowboy. I don't know how else to show them."

"Why do they need to know I'm a cowboy? After all, I'm really not."

"We're creating an illusion, Russ," she huffed. "Women love cowboys, especially Wyoming cowboys. And for Wyoming Bright, there's no other kind."

"Yeah, but what I can't figure is why women love cowboys. I mean, they're around horses and cows all day. They smell. A lot of cowboys don't have good manners, are loners. What makes a cowboy so special?"

To his surprise, Melissa sat beside him on the top step after lifting the stroller on to the porch. She left plenty of space between them, so Mandy would feel part of the group, but at least she was near him once again. "I think the cowboy represents the knight of medieval times," she explained. "Strong, protective, handsome, one man against evil."

He stared at her, stunned by her poetic portrait. "Is that how you saw your fiancé?"

She stiffened. "Greg has nothing to do with what

we're doing. He wasn't a cowboy. That's why he thought I should bid on one at the auction.''

"So it was his idea?''

"We agreed.''

"You could've hired a real cowboy for a whole lot less, Melissa.''

"But I wouldn't have gotten the publicity I'm going to get.''

"What publicity? You mean you're going to tell people I sat in a bubble bath and had my picture taken?''

"Of course.''

He leaped to his feet. "Now, wait just a minute! You can't do that.''

"The Casper newspaper has run a story on each bachelor from the auction. The reporter will be over Sunday to interview you and me about our weekend.'' She paused, then added, "Besides, if your picture is going to be in every card shop in Wyoming, what difference does it make if it's in the paper?''

"Because my name will be under the picture. I don't care if a bunch of tourists buy the cards. They'll never know who I am. But I still have friends in Casper. I don't want them to open the paper and stare at me in the altogether with a bunch of bubbles.''

She stood, too. "They won't see anything but your chest—that's the reason for the bubbles. And you've certainly shown off your chest before.''

She had a point, but he didn't want to agree with

her. "Maybe so, but being in a bathtub, *looking* like I'm naked, makes people believe it."

"But you won't be naked, since you brought your swimsuit with you." She put her hands on her trim hips, as if challenging him.

Before he could come up with a response, the door to the store opened and Sam and an older boy each carried out two buckets of water.

"One of you better go get them bubbles. This here water is gonna cool off mighty quick." Sam stared at Russ, a grin on his face. "I'm thinking a cold bath wouldn't hurt you, Russ, boy, but you might not find it too comfortable."

Russ watched the blood rush to Melissa's cheeks, but unfortunately, he could feel his own face growing hot, too. "Forget it, Sam," he growled.

The old man took no offense. As he got ready to pour one of the buckets into the tub, he warned, "Better move the baby back. We don't want any hot water to splash on her."

Russ immediately wheeled the stroller to the other side of the porch before Melissa could make a move. Then he knelt down beside the baby.

"Hey, Mandy, you be a good girl while I help your mommy, and later we'll play."

She cooed and jumped, as if trying to reach him, and he chuckled in return. He really was enjoying the little girl. Somehow it had never occurred to him that he would.

"I'll take care of my daughter," Melissa said crisply, frowning at him.

"Nope, you have to be getting your gear ready. Like Sam said, that water's going to get cold, and I'm not staying in it long."

He left her staring at him, her anger rising, and walked into the store to find the bubble stuff the boys had told him about. Not knowing how much he would need, he took about six bottles out to the porch.

"Should I just pour it in?" he asked.

Melissa didn't bother to answer, and Sam shrugged his shoulders.

Russ opened a bottle and poured it in. Nothing happened. "This isn't working!"

The two boys arrived back at the porch with a couple of towels just in time to hear Russ's complaint.

"You have to make the bubbles by splashing the water," one of them said. He leaned over and swirled his hand in the water. "Like this."

A few bubbles appeared, but definitely not enough to cover up his swimsuit. "I think I'm going to need some help. While I pour the goop in, you two stir the water and make bubbles. Okay?"

That plan worked fairly well. Russ finished those six bottles and got four more out of the store. He didn't want to run out of bubbles.

Then he sat down on the steps and removed his boots, as he'd intended to do earlier. Next came his shirt.

"You can't strip out here!" Melissa protested.

Aha. She was watching him. He looked at her, a

smile on his lips. "Don't worry. I'm going inside to change. You ready to take some pictures?"

She didn't look enthusiastic, but she nodded. "You'd better hurry. I think Sam was right about the water cooling."

"Maybe you should be the one getting in the tub," Russ suggested with a grin.

She ignored him.

"Quit your teasin', boy, and hurry up," Sam warned. "Them bubbles are already disappearin'."

Inside the store, Russ stripped off his jeans and underwear and pulled on his modest swim trunks. Then he grabbed the towels he'd need when the shoot was finished. That bubble stuff looked pretty slimy. When he stepped outside, he noted Melissa's assessing look before she turned away.

"Will this do?" he asked, imitating a runway model. When Melissa ignored him, he dropped the towels nearby. The boys giggled at his behavior.

He was concentrating on catching Melissa's attention as he swung one foot into the tub. When he lifted his other foot, the one in the tub slid out from under him. He sat down hard, a tidal wave of bubbles slopping over the sides.

"Gol darn it, boy! What are you doing? We lost half our bubbles," Sam protested.

"This stuff is slippery as all get out," Russ snapped, embarrassed at his awkwardness.

"Come on, Jimmy, let's get some more buckets of water. You two better get some more bubble stuff."

As the other four males disappeared, Melissa asked, "Did you hurt yourself?"

"I think I bruised my tailbone, which should make riding a real pleasure," he growled.

"I tried to—never mind." She crossed over behind the tub and picked up his Stetson where it had fallen. Placing it willy-nilly on his head, she backed away.

"What do you want me to do?" he asked.

Seemingly her good humor was restored. "Smile. Tilt your hat back, rest your arms on the edges of the tub and smile."

MELISSA DREW A DEEP BREATH as Russ displayed his muscles for the camera. The man's arms looked rock hard. "You must work out all the time," she murmured as she eyed him through the lens. She was much more comfortable talking to him when she had the camera between them, as if it shielded her from his sex appeal.

"Yeah. Architecture doesn't build muscles."

"Did you ever work as a carpenter?" She'd found her models were more relaxed if she got them talking. After taking several pictures, she decided to change his position.

"Yeah, when I was in school. That's how I paid for food. I worked every summer building houses."

"Okay, cross your arms over your chest and tilt your head down, as if you're napping. Pull the hat down over your eyes."

He did as she asked. The midafternoon sun was

shining on him, since the porch faced west, and she felt sure the pictures would be even better than she'd hoped.

"Here's more water," Sam announced as he and his troops returned. "Now, don't get the hat wet, boys, 'cause it's mine."

They poured in more water.

"Ow! That's hot," Russ protested

"Wait!" Melissa called. She pointed to the smallest boy. "What's your name?"

"Danny," he said shyly, grinning.

"Danny, would you pour the water in while I take a picture? Just you and Russ?"

The boy beamed. "I get to be in the picture?"

"If you don't mind. I'll pay you—" She broke off as she saw the envy in the other boys' eyes. "I'll pay all of you for helping, of course. But since Danny is so small compared to Russ and the tub, it makes a cute picture. I just wish he had suspenders."

"Got some in the store," Sam announced. He went inside and immediately returned with a pair to fit Danny.

"That store is marvelous, Sam." Melissa had forgotten her disgruntlement over Russ insisting on the tub pictures. She was seeing her earlier vision come alive before her eyes, and it was just what she wanted.

After Danny had his suspenders in place, everyone else moved back and he got ready to pour the water.

"Russ, please watch Danny and pretend to be washing your arm."

She had the other boy, whose name turned out to be Tom, to kneel behind Russ and pretend to scrub his back, while Russ looked over his shoulder as if to supervise.

Then she had the three boys and Sam all sit in chairs lining the porch, tipping them back against the wall, with Russ in the foreground.

"I want—Russ, smear some bubbles on your chest."

The water came just a little above his waist and she wanted some variation, as if he'd scrubbed his chest with the soap bubbles. He frowned and dipped his hand for a few bubbles.

"No, no, I need more bubbles," she said, frowning. She strode over to the tub and plunged her hand into the warm water, scooping up a lot of bubbles.

Then she rubbed them over his chest.

Suddenly she jerked her hand away. His muscles had tensed under her touch, and she'd liked the feel of them much more than she should have.

She hurriedly took a couple of more pictures, then excused her model. "I think that's enough of this shot. You can go get dressed."

Her camera bag was near the tub and she crossed the porch to bend down and get a new roll of film. She heard Russ stirring the water as he got up, but she kept her back to him.

He reached for one of the towels and dripped water on her.

"Hey!" she protested, standing. She was about to protest more when her gaze fell on him—and she got another idea.

CHAPTER SEVEN

"WAIT," MELISSA CALLED. Russ stopped toweling off his chest and raised one brow. "I didn't drip on you on purpose," he protested.

"It's not that." She looked away for a moment, then turned to face him squarely. "I'm going to take advantage of you again. I want to take some more pictures."

"Right. I know. On horseback." He kept his gaze pinned on her delicate features.

"No, I want more pictures now." She stepped over to him and removed the Stetson. "Sam, why don't you hold your hat until we go to the barn so it won't get messed up."

Russ said nothing, waiting for Melissa to explain what she wanted. In the meantime, all he could think about was whether her taking advantage of him meant he could kiss her again. The softness of her lips, her sweetness, even her quick wit, made a kiss so desirable, he couldn't think of anything else.

Which probably explained why he didn't realize Melissa was already snapping pictures.

"How will they know I'm a cowboy if I'm not

wearing the Stetson?'' he asked, giving her a side-ways grin to tease her.

The camera clicked again.

"Doesn't matter," she muttered. "Wrap the towel around you."

He looped it around his neck, holding both ends in his hands.

After several snaps of the camera, she gave more directions. "Wrap it around your waist."

"Ms. Bright, you want women to believe I'm naked beneath this towel?" he asked in mock horror. Before she could answer, however, he did as she asked.

She walked around him, taking pictures from different angles. Then she paused, studying him. When she moved in close, he drew a deep breath, appreciating the scent of her—flowers and a touch of spice. In fact, he was enjoying himself, perfectly relaxed, until her warm fingers slid over his skin, pushing down the towel and swimsuit an inch or two.

"What are you doing?" he demanded as his body tensed at her touch.

"Adding a little suspense to the picture. Women will be wondering if your towel is about to fall off."

He cocked an eyebrow again. "And this is a good thing?" As he finished his question, she snapped another picture.

"Oh, yes," she assured him, her voice husky. "Put your eyebrow up again. I like that."

"I aim to please," he assured her.

"That's a first," Sam informed Melissa. "As a boy he was an ornery cuss."

"Now, Sam," Russ protested, "let's not give away any secrets."

The boys giggled, covering their mouths with their hands when Russ pretended to glare at them. "Don't tell me all of you are perfect angels."

They all nodded, their laughter growing, and Melissa took a picture of them, too. Then she looked at Russ. "You can go clean up. I think I'll take some more pictures of these guys, if they don't mind."

"Ah, training them early to be beefcake models? Okay, but, boys, don't let her talk you into stripping for her."

The boys protested, but the loudest protest came from Melissa. "Russ Hall! You know I wouldn't do that!"

"Just checking," he assured her with a wink before he strode off in the direction of Sam's cabin to take a shower.

Maybe another cold one.

Melissa relaxed once Russ left the porch. She posed Sam and the boys for different shots, causing a lot of laughter when she had them make a pyramid by stacking them on their hands and knees. When the pyramid collapsed, the boys rolled around on the grass laughing.

"Hey," the youngest boy, Danny, called when Mandy shrieked. "Can we make a picture with the baby?"

Until Russ had mentioned pictures with Mandy,

Melissa had never considered using her baby as a model. With a shrug, she agreed with the boy's request.

"Sure. I think she feels left out."

Each boy had his picture taken holding Mandy. Then Sam wanted his turn. Melissa couldn't help but think about her little girl growing up an only child, as she had done. Russ might not have had parents around, but he'd had surrogate brothers, as these boys did.

Mandy was enjoying all the attention. When Russ returned, however, she beamed at him and clapped her hands.

"Howdy, Miss Sunshine," he said, reaching for her.

Mandy grabbed his nose and gurgled with laughter. Melissa couldn't resist snapping a shot of the two of them. They both turned to look at her, surprise on their faces, and she took another picture.

Russ grinned at her. "You changed your mind about Mandy modeling?"

Melissa smiled. "Why not? She's cheap labor. All I have to do is keep her supplied with teething biscuits."

"Hey, have you tried paying these guys with teething biscuits?" he suggested, heading toward the boys.

They all protested. Melissa hurriedly assured them she intended to use real money to pay them for their services. She put down her camera and reached for her camera bag, pulling out her billfold. The boys' eyes widened as she offered them cash.

AN HOUR LATER, Russ was once again dressed like a cowboy, Sam's Stetson on his head. They had moved to the barn for the pictures on horseback.

Sam, having surrendered a happy Mandy to Melissa, came out of the barn leading a large horse. "How about Jack, Melissa? Will he do?"

"He'll do just fine, if you mean the horse, Sam. Thank you." She turned to Russ. "Is this horse all right with you?"

"Sure."

Russ crossed over to Sam and took the reins from him. Then he stepped into the stirrup and swung himself into the saddle. He'd hoped to impress Melissa with his grace, but the sudden pain he felt had him collapsing against the saddle with all the grace of a grade-A klutz.

Which didn't help the bruise on his tailbone.

"Are you all right?" she asked, taking a step closer but still keeping her distance. She held Mandy in her arms.

"A little sore from the bubble bath escapade," he said. "Why don't you bring Mandy over. She can have her first riding lesson."

"No! That would be dangerous."

"No it wouldn't. Tell her, Sam."

"Old Jack is tame as they come, Melissa. Mandy would like it."

"Want to come for a ride, Mandy?" Russ called, clapping his hands and holding them out to her baby.

Mandy practically leaped out of her arms, trying to reach Russ.

"See, she wants to ride. Hand her up."

"No, I won't."

"But you promised to take a couple of pictures of me and Mandy together. This will be perfect." He wasn't sure why he wanted more pictures of him and the baby so badly, but he did.

When she still hesitated, he pointed out that the horse hadn't moved a muscle since he'd mounted it. "It really is safe, Melissa. I wouldn't suggest you do anything that would harm Mandy."

Triumph filled him when Melissa walked toward him. He liked thinking she trusted him. Mandy reached eagerly for him when Melissa held her up. He took the baby and cradled her against him with one arm.

"See, Mandy? You're taking your first ride." He slowly guided the horse in a circle. Melissa's anxious face amused him, but it also touched him. She cared so deeply for her child.

"Ready to take some pictures?" he asked.

Without comment, she stepped closer and snapped several photos of him and Mandy. "Now, give her to me. I'd like to finish while the sun sets. Some silhouette pictures. Besides, both Mandy and I are getting tired."

"Right. Sam, come take Mandy."

"I'll take her," Melissa insisted.

"You can't hold her and shoot at the same time," Russ argued, giving the baby to Sam, who held her as naturally as any mother.

"Thank you, Sam," Melissa said, but she was frowning.

Russ tried several times to tease a smile from her, but he couldn't. Suddenly, she was all business, directing him into the poses she wanted.

The last stance was on a rise, so Russ was silhouetted against the glorious colors of the sunset.

"There, that should do it," she said with a sigh. "Thank you, Russ, and you, too, Sam. You were such a help."

"Happy to help a lady," Sam said with a smile. "I should say two ladies. This little one is getting hungry again, though. It's a good thing you've finished."

Russ swung down from the horse, wincing at the sudden movement. He'd grown stiff sitting in the saddle. "Uh, I'll go unsaddle the horse and then we can go," he told Melissa.

"You go ahead, boy," Sam ordered. "This little one won't wait."

After more expressions of their appreciation, and a few minutes packing up all the equipment into the little car, Russ strapped Mandy into the baby seat in back.

"Why don't I drive, Melissa? You seem a little tired."

"I suspect you are, too. Modeling is much harder than it looks, and you were superb today. I'm going to drop the film off as soon as we get back to town and we'll have the results tomorrow.''

"That soon?"

"Yes, I'll put a rush on it. But if you don't mind driving…"

He opened the passenger door and waited for her to get in.

As she settled into the seat, she said, "Are you sure you don't mind driving? I feel terrible letting you do it when you must be just as exhausted.'' She started to get out again.

"I'm driving," he said firmly, and closed the car door.

When he slid behind the wheel, she was still prepared to argue. He put an end to it when he said, "I know you usually manage very well on your own, but now that I'm here, I can help."

She fell silent.

"You have a problem letting people help you, don't you?"

Her head snapped around and she stared at him. "Probably so. There haven't been a lot of offers.''

Her words bothered him. He thought again of his mother, a teenager, alone with a baby. Had no one offered to help her? Had she, too, been totally alone?

Not that Melissa was completely alone. She had Mrs. Tuttle to watch over Mandy sometimes. But that's when she was working. Did she ever take time for herself?

A sudden idea struck him. He'd only met Melissa twenty-four hours earlier, but he'd quickly come to admire her determination, her hard work, her loving care of Mandy. Even more, he was growing increasingly attracted to her, which wasn't necessarily a good thing, he reminded himself.

But he wanted to do something for her, and now he knew what. It would take a little maneuvering, but he'd manage.

"TURN RIGHT AT THE NEXT corner," Melissa directed from the passenger seat. It was so strange to have someone drive her. "Stop at the red sign. I'll hop out and run the film in. If there isn't a parking place, you can circle the block."

"Sure. But you'd better hurry. I think Mandy's appetite is going to take over any moment."

She looked over her shoulder at her daughter. Mandy's pacifier had fallen to her tummy and was caught against the baby seat. Melissa reached for it and stuck it back in her mouth. "Maybe that will hold her for a few minutes."

Hurrying into the film shop, she gave her instructions and was promised the results by two o'clock the next day. When she stepped back outside, Russ and Mandy were waiting, blocking one lane with the emergency flashers going.

Melissa slipped into the car. "You might've gotten a ticket. Why didn't you circle the block?"

"I didn't want you to wait. I know you're tired and I figured it wouldn't take you long." He smiled, and Melissa shivered. His voice and smile held such warmth, a caressing tone that eased her stress and made her feel protected.

A dangerous feeling.

She cleared her throat. "Well, thanks. Now we'll head home and I'll have dinner on the table shortly. I'm sure you're starving."

"Nope."

"You're not?" she asked, surprised. The man could put away an enormous amount of food.

"Oh, I'm starving, but I don't want you cooking. There's a good barbecue place close by, if I remember right, and we're going to pick up dinner there."

"That's thoughtful, but I used all my cash on the boys at the ranch. I suppose I can charge..." she said, thinking aloud.

"Nope," he repeated. "I'm buying."

"No, you spent all day working for me. I'm not letting you pay for dinner."

"Melissa, would you just listen for once. Dinner is on me. Now, stop arguing and lean back and relax."

She glared at him and remained rigidly upright in her seat until she realized she was being foolish and ungrateful.

She was tired. The creativity involved in photography always exhausted her, and today had been burdened with a lot of emotional baggage. She couldn't look at Russ as some mere acquaintance, with no meaning in her life. And that scared her.

"Hey, they've added a drive-through," Russ exclaimed as he turned into the parking lot of Roy's Barbecue, a long-established restaurant in Casper.

"Yes, they put it in about five years ago. It makes it easy to pick up a meal." She'd driven through a few times this past year when she was too tired to even think of cooking.

"Know what you want?"

She gave him her preferences, then listened as he ordered the food, about four times as much as she'd told him. "I hope you're the one who's going to eat all that food," she muttered.

He chuckled. "I was going to say I'm hungry enough to eat a horse, but in deference to Jack, I'll change that to hungry enough to eat a bear."

Mandy chose that moment to let the adults know that Russ wasn't the only one who was hungry. She let out a wail that caught both of them off guard.

"Wow, that kid has a siren of a scream, doesn't she?"

"She's learning to be assertive," Melissa corrected him. "Girls need to learn how to make demands."

"I think she's got it down pat," Russ assured her, grinning.

The man at the drive-through window claimed his attention then, and Melissa tried to soothe Mandy.

Ten minutes later, they reached her home. She unstrapped Mandy and carried her in, telling Russ to leave the equipment until after they'd eaten. He brought in the food without comment.

"I need to change Mandy and then feed her, but

you go ahead and eat. There are some sodas in the fridge.''

Without waiting for his agreement, she hurried down the hall toward Mandy's room. A few minutes later, she had Mandy's diaper changed and a clean T-shirt replacing the stained one. Melissa carried her baby into the kitchen, expecting to find Russ at the table.

Instead, the room was empty. Frowning, Melissa settled Mandy in her high chair. Then she opened the refrigerator and took out a bottle she had prepared the day before. She uncapped it and put it in the microwave, then took jars of English peas and carrots from a shelf.

Just as she settled herself at the table to feed Mandy, she heard the front door open. ''Russ?'' she called.

''Yeah? You need something? I'll be right there.''

After several bumps she couldn't identify, he appeared at the kitchen door.

''What are you doing?'' she asked. ''Why aren't you eating? You said you were starving.''

''I am, but I imagine you are, too. I thought I'd unload the car while you take care of Mandy. Then we can eat together.''

''But I was going to unload later. You're a guest. You don't have to—''

''No, I'm not a guest. I'm—I'm your partner for the weekend.'' He turned around and disappeared out the door.

Just as well. Melissa was in shock. *Her partner?*

He was taking Greg's place? Everything within her rebelled at the thought. No, no, no. Mandy belonged to her and Greg. There would never be anyone to replace him.

She drew a deep breath and calmed down. Russ hadn't meant those words as they'd sounded. He was here as a—a helper. That's what she'd intended, and he was certainly living up to the bargain.

He reentered the kitchen. "What do you want to drink with your meal?" he asked as he opened the refrigerator.

"I can get it later. I—"

"What do you want to drink?" he asked, this time in an irritated tone.

She stared at him, confused. "Why are you upset?"

"Because I'm getting tired of you refusing to let me do anything. I don't have to be waited on hand and foot. I can help out occasionally."

"You've helped me all day long, Russ. There's no need to wait on *me*."

"You're making this a lot more difficult than it has to be. What do you want to drink?"

"A diet soda will be fine," she said, ducking her head to avoid his stare.

After getting drinks out of the refrigerator, he opened a cupboard and took down two glasses and filled them with ice, then poured the sodas in them. He set one near her and the other across the table.

Mandy bounced in her high chair and pounded on the tray.

"Hey, little girl, did I forget to say hello?" he asked, leaning down to the child, his voice warm and sweet. "Are you getting enough to eat? I'll share my barbecue, if you want."

"I think barbecue is a little advanced for her," Melissa advised him, not knowing if he was teasing or not. He shot her a superior look that told her he was.

"Right. So maybe I should cook her a steak?"

"Just sit down and eat, Russ." She was too tired to think of a snappy comeback tonight.

"I'll eat when you eat. We're partners today, Melissa."

She gave up. If he wanted to deny himself the pleasure of dinner until she ate, so be it. Though considering the quantity he'd bought, it wouldn't hurt him to get a head start.

When Mandy had almost finished her vegetables, he asked, "Doesn't she get a bottle? Want me to fix it?"

"I put it in the microwave."

"I'll get it." He jumped up from the table and then grimaced.

"Your tailbone still hurts? Sit down. I'll get the bottle. You probably should be sitting in a soft chair. If you want to eat in the den, I can—"

"I'm fine," he assured her. "It's not as if I broke something. I'll get the bottle." He retrieved the bottle, screwing on the lid and nipple.

"Ba-ba-ba-ba," Mandy gurgled, reaching for the bottle as he came back to the table.

"Ah. A popular item, huh, Mandy? Want Uncle Russ to give it to you? Come on, baby, and I'll feed you." He set the bottle on the table and reached for her daughter.

"Wait—" Melissa began in protest.

"Melissa, quit trying to do everything yourself. Let me help," he insisted, impatience in his voice. Before she could say anything else, he lifted Mandy from her high chair and crossed to his chair, reaching for her bottle as he sat down. Mandy, in her excitement, grabbed his face and promptly smeared carrots and peas all over his cheek.

"Eeeew!" he protested.

Melissa offered no sympathy. "I was going to say you should wait until I'd cleaned her hands and face, but you had to have your way. Serves you right."

CHAPTER EIGHT

HOLDING ON TO MANDY'S hands so she couldn't do further damage, he looked at Melissa. "I thought you were being difficult about letting me help. Seems like you turn down every offer I make."

"No, I don't. But it takes a little getting used to, having someone around." She remained seated, her face calm.

"I wouldn't turn down a little help now," he ventured. "If you want to clean Mandy or bring me a paper towel, I'd appreciate it."

For a minute, he thought she was going to refuse to move. But he should've known better. Melissa was a nurturer. With a nod, she grabbed a clean dishcloth and wet it at the sink. Then she came around the table and wiped first one little hand and then the other.

Mandy smiled, undisturbed by her mother's attention. After wiping her daughter's face, Melissa turned her attention to Russ.

"Do you want me to clean you, too?"

"Yeah, if there's a clean spot left on the towel."

Her fingers settled on his chin, lifting his face toward the light. He liked her touch, soft, warm. When she finished wiping off the vegetables Mandy had deposited on his cheek, he almost leaned forward to kiss her. As a thank-you, of course, nothing more.

Her closeness, her personal attention made another kiss seem like a natural. But he'd already made that mistake once today. If he kissed her again, he'd find himself in a hotel, for sure.

"Uh, thanks," he muttered as she moved back. He noticed her cheeks were flushed, which told him she was as disturbed by their closeness as he was.

"Do you want me to feed Mandy her bottle?" she offered again.

"No. I'll do it. Why don't you fix our plates before the food gets cold."

Without saying anything, she began to do as he asked. When she'd put a plate with several sandwiches in front of him, she said, "Mandy is perfectly capable of holding her own bottle if you can eat with one hand."

"Really?" He stared at the baby. Her hands were on either side of the bottle, but he hadn't realized she could manage without his help. Turning the bottle loose, he watched it sag momentarily before the baby lifted it herself. "Well, I'll be. I didn't know you were that talented, Mandy, my girl."

"She can already do a lot of things for herself," Melissa said with a sad air.

"That doesn't make you happy?"

"Oh, of course it does, but—but she's changing and growing so quickly. She'll be my only baby and I want to hold on to the sweetness of this first year."

He'd been about to take a bite out of one of the sandwiches, but he put it back on the plate. "What do you mean, she'll be your only baby. Can't you have more children?"

She seemed startled by his question. "I suppose— I mean, physically, I could, but—well, one needs a husband to have more children."

His gaze roamed her trim figure, her beautiful face. "I shouldn't think you'd have any trouble finding a husband."

"I'm not looking!" she snapped.

"But you should."

"Oh, that's rich. A confirmed bachelor is urging *me* to marry?"

He opened his mouth to respond, then shut it. She had a point. Then he thought of an important reason she should consider another marriage. "But you have Mandy. She needs a dad."

He could tell he'd hit a nerve. Melissa stiffened and looked away. "She'll be all right. You'd better eat your sandwiches before they grow cold."

"You haven't eaten yours, either."

"No, I've been too busy arguing with you." She immediately took a bite and industriously chewed as if her life depended on it. Russ did the same, but he kept thinking about their conversation. Why wouldn't Melissa consider marriage?

He didn't want Mandy missing out on a two-parent family. After watching *Leave It to Beaver* and other sitcoms, maybe he had an unrealistic view of families, but he knew how lonely he'd sometimes felt.

How different he'd been from the kids at school who had fathers and mothers.

Looking at the sweet face resting on his chest, he felt a surge of protectiveness that was new to him. He'd only been in Casper twenty-four hours, but he could already tell he was forming an attachment to the baby.

And her mother.

Maybe it was because they had brought back thoughts of his own mother. He didn't know. His stay had definitely given him a different perspective on his own childhood. But he wanted the best for Melissa Bright. Maybe he should look up some old friends, try to find a man for her. Someone to take her out, make her feel special, spend some time with Mandy. Someone who wanted to make a family.

He didn't know anyone like that.

He'd made a point of making friends with confirmed bachelors like himself. Besides, it would take a special man to weave his way into Melissa's life.

"Da-da-da-da," Mandy cooed at him.

"No!" Melissa almost shouted, coming up out of her chair.

"What?" Russ demanded, shocked out of his thoughts. He stared at the baby, afraid he'd done something wrong.

The loud voices had Mandy's smile disappearing and an alarmed expression crossed her face.

"She—she doesn't know what she's saying," Melissa hurriedly mumbled, subsiding back into her chair.

Russ stared at the baby and then the mother. "I think she's trying to tell me she's finished her bottle." He set the bottle on the table and eased Mandy onto his shoulder. "I burp her, right?"

"Yes." She had her gaze on her sandwich, as if she was embarrassed.

He knew what the problem was, of course, but he wasn't going to admit it. He didn't want to get into an argument with Melissa because Mandy had babbled something that sounded very much like daddy. After all, he'd been shocked that morning when she'd done so. But she wasn't calling him daddy.

Because she didn't know anything about a daddy...yet.

When she let out her normal loud burp, Russ eased her back to his lap. And discovered Melissa standing beside him. "I'll put her back in her high chair while we finish eating."

"Won't she fuss?"

"No, I'll give her a teething biscuit." She whisked the baby over to the high chair.

"When will her other teeth come in? I mean, I've seen four, but she's got a way to go, doesn't she?"

"Yes. She's cutting some, now. But she won't have a full mouth of teeth for another year, I guess." She found the teething biscuit and removed the cellophane from it. Then she put it on the tray of Mandy's chair and let her pick it up by herself. The baby immediately grabbed it and tried to stuff the whole cookie in her mouth.

"Wow. It's a good thing her mouth is small," Russ said before he took another bite.

"Yes," Melissa agreed.

Little was said after that, each of the adults concentrating on eating their meal and Mandy chewing away on her teething biscuit.

Russ helped clear the table when they'd finished, but Melissa still didn't say a word.

When that task was completed, he looked at Melissa. "What else do you have to do?"

"I'm going to fold some clothes. You can watch television or read. You might want to look at the newspaper. It's in the living room."

"Or I might want to fold clothes."

"Not necessary." Her tones were clipped.

He took Mandy out of the high chair *after* Melissa had cleaned her up. He'd at least learned that lesson. Then he followed Melissa to the small laundry behind the kitchen. She gathered a load of dry clothes and took them to the sofa in the living room.

"What does Mandy do while you're working?"

"I put her in her playpen with toys. That keeps her happy for a while." After answering him, Melissa left the room again.

He didn't know where she was going, so he decided to put Mandy in her playpen. Once he'd set her down on the soft surface, she lunged for a bright red-and-yellow ball, carrying it immediately to her mouth. Since the ball was as big as her little face, he didn't have to worry about her swallowing it.

Melissa came back in and sat on the sofa, reaching for the nearest piece of baby clothing.

Russ moved to the other end of the sofa, shoving some of the clothing aside so he could sit. Then he, too, picked up a baby T-shirt.

"What are you doing?" Melissa asked.

"Helping you."

"I don't need your help," she insisted.

"I thought that was why I was here? You wanted me to play daddy for the weekend." He waited, curious, for her response.

"Not—not daddy. I just wanted to sleep late one morning. I wanted—I didn't mean you had to do everything." Again her cheeks were flushed.

He settled back against the sofa cushion, staring at her. "You know, Melissa, I'm beginning to think you're one of those people I detest."

MELISSA WAS SURPRISED at how much his words hurt. She jerked her head up and stared at him, fighting not to reveal her pain. "What kind of people?"

"The kind who complain about their problems but refuse to do anything about them. They luxuriate in them, actually. I believe they're called martyrs."

She blinked rapidly to hold back the tears that suddenly filled her eyes. Then, biting her bottom lip, she reached over to gather all the clothes to be folded. Without a word, she walked from the room, her arms filled with the laundry. After putting them in the rocker in Mandy's room, she returned and scooped the baby out of the playpen.

"What are you doing?" Russ asked.

"I'm taking Mandy to her room."

"Why?"

"Because I don't want her to disturb you." She tried to get out of the room before he could ask any more questions. She didn't want to talk to the annoying man. But he stood and came after her.

"She's not bothering me."

She said nothing. When she reached Mandy's room, she crossed over to the crib and put Mandy inside. Then she collected several toys from a shelf, a stuffed tiger and a smaller ball with stars on it, and put them in the bed with her child.

As she turned to the rocker to start folding the clothes, Russ, standing in the door, said, "I guess I hurt your feelings."

"Don't be ridiculous. The television is in the living room. Or if you want to go out, feel free to take my car. The keys are—I don't know where the keys are. You had them last." She didn't want to talk about how badly he'd hurt her.

She'd worked hard to provide a happy environment for her baby after Greg's death. Too often as a child she'd listened to her mother whine about the unfairness of life, and she'd vowed not to be so negative in her own life. Now Russ was accusing her of just that.

"I know where the keys are, but I'm not going anywhere."

"Suit yourself," she said, turning her back on him.

She almost jumped out of her skin when his warm hands closed on her shoulders.

"What are you doing?" she demanded, yanking herself out of his grasp.

"I didn't mean to hurt your feelings."

But he had. She hated martyrs. She'd had no intention of becoming one. But her innate honesty made her question whether he was right.

And it scared her.

The last thing she wanted was to fail Mandy and Greg. To be less than the best parent she could be. But a martyr wouldn't be the best parent. Her own mother had played that role too often for Melissa not to abhor it.

She couldn't do that to Mandy. *Dear God, please.*

"It doesn't matter."

"Yes, it does," Russ contradicted her. "You've been a great hostess. I want to fulfill my obligation. But I'm getting frustrated. Every time I offer to help, you'd think I was going to steal the crown jewels."

"You're right, of course," she assured him, her voice breathless. She was in pain. To prove to this man, and herself, that she hadn't become like her mother, she was going to have to accept every offer he made, and smile while doing so.

"It was silly of me to resist. I—I didn't want to work you too hard." She attempted a chuckle, as if their situation was funny. "I was afraid you'd run out on me."

"If I promise to stay, can I help fold the laundry?"

She took one quick glance at the sincerity in his

blue eyes and looked away. "Of course. You probably fold laundry all the time in Chicago. I—I just hadn't pictured a swinging bachelor doing chores like that."

He moved to the rocker and, after watching her fold a sleeper, grabbed one just like it and imitated her. Then he laid it on top of the dresser where she'd put the one she folded.

"Nicely done, thank you," she said, attempting to be scrupulously polite.

"Are you going to thank me for each thing I fold?" he asked, a grin on his face.

She ground her teeth, holding on to her temper by a thread. Didn't he realize she was trying to— This was ridiculous, she suddenly realized.

"I'll probably write you a thank-you note," she said, relaxing a little, "since I'm so surprised."

"Only one? I'd expect one for each item," he informed her, rewarding her attempt at a joke with an even warmer smile.

She smiled back but speeded up her folding. The sooner they finished the task, the happier she'd be. His closeness brought too many memories, made her ask herself too many questions.

When it sounded as if Mandy had called him daddy, every part of her being had protested. But did she want Mandy to be without a daddy all her life because Greg had died? To be an only child, without brothers or sisters?

Of course she didn't. But for Mandy to have a daddy, she'd have to have a husband. Russ had already shown her she could respond to another man. But Russ wasn't a good prospect for a husband. He was a confirmed bachelor, albeit a kind one, one who was gentle with Mandy.

As a lover, he would be…perfect, she admitted as a shiver ran through her body.

Enough! She couldn't think of the man in those terms and get through the next two days without embarrassing herself. As it was, she was going to have to accept his help.

Maybe she could think of him as the brother she never had.

She looked at him out of the corner of her eye and dismissed that idea as ridiculous.

DAMN, HE'D ALMOST BLOWN IT. Russ hadn't meant to be so hard on her, but his frustration had overpowered his good sense.

And he'd hurt her.

He'd seen those tears in her eyes. She'd tried to hide them, but he'd seen them. At least she seemed to have recovered, which gave him an enormous sense of relief. Melissa had a good sense of humor, but he hadn't been sure it could overcome his ugly remark.

They finished folding the clothes in no time. Melissa put them away and he didn't offer to help. After all, he didn't know where they belonged, though he watched her carefully so he'd know where to find things in the morning.

"What now?"

She gave him a guarded look, as if wondering whether she could refuse his help. He kept a smile on his face.

"I need to prepare more bottles."

"Maybe Mandy and I will just watch you. I think I'd probably get in your way in the kitchen."

"She can sit in her high chair," she offered, "if you have something else you want to do."

"Nope. I'd like to play with her. It's a novelty, remember?"

She nodded before lifting Mandy from the bed and handing her to him. They'd come a long way from last night, when she was reluctant to let him touch Mandy.

When they reached the kitchen, he sat down at the table, Mandy in his lap. "Do you play any of those baby games with her?"

"Baby games?"

"You know, this Little Pig Went to Market, or Ride a Little Horsey?"

She stared at him. "I thought you didn't know anything about babies?"

"I don't, not really. But I remember some from— I guess from the ranch." He frowned. He hadn't been around babies much at the ranch. Most of the boys were older when they came there. Where had he heard those rhymes?

"I probably learned them from television."

"Or maybe your mother—"

"No!"

Mandy let out a little sob, alarmed by his sharp

tones. He cuddled her against him, soothing her. More calmly, he added, "No, I don't remember anything about my mother."

"Really? I thought you were taken to the ranch when you were four," Melissa commented as she opened a can of formula and began pouring it into the bottles.

"I was, but I don't remember anything before then." He'd never tried to remember. The sound of a soft voice played in his head, chanting Ride a Little Horsey. Was that Mrs. Duncan? Had he heard her playing with one of the other boys?

"Yes, I play those games with her," Melissa said, a sad look on her face as she stared at him.

At least she'd stopped asking him questions he didn't like.

"Okay, Mandy, we'll make a cowgirl out of you yet." He sat the baby on one knee, his hands around her tubby little middle, and bounced her gently while he chanted the rhyme. At the end, he lifted her into the air and she squealed, a beaming smile on her face.

"I thought she was supposed to fall down, not fly up," Melissa said with a smile.

"I learned it this way, and Mandy likes it," he told her with pride. "Let's go again, sweetheart."

For half an hour, he and Mandy played together while Melissa prepared the bottles then mixed muffins for breakfast the next morning. When she'd finished, she checked the pantry and refrigerator and made a grocery list.

"You're pretty organized," he commented as Mandy subsided against him, chuckling.

Melissa smiled at her baby. "You've really entertained her. I've never heard her laugh so much."

"Me, neither. She's a real sweetheart."

"Yes, she is," Melissa agreed as she turned back to her list.

"So we'll go grocery shopping tomorrow?"

She opened her mouth and Russ could see the protest coming. He held his breath, not wanting to fight with her again.

"Well, I'll go. You can come if you want, if you don't have anything else to do."

"Nope. Mandy and I will be happy to go with you. Besides, we can get the tire on your car repaired at the same time."

His smile broadened when she nodded without protesting. Good. She was willing to accept his help.

"Do you go to the mall much? I noticed they'd built one near the photography store."

"I visit the stores that carry our cards occasionally. You know, to see how things are selling, to ask them for ideas. They're the ones who encouraged me to focus on cowboys, as well as the mountains."

"Do you travel to all the shops that carry your cards?"

"No," she said with a chuckle. "My cards are sold all over Wyoming. I'd never get any work done if I did that. Though, when I got my first order, I drove almost a hundred miles to hand-deliver them, just so I could see them in a store."

A reminiscent smile curved her lips and he thought she'd never looked more beautiful.

"I understand," he assured her. "I felt the same way about the first building I'd designed that was actually built. For weeks, I drove out of my way to work just so I could pass by it."

They smiled in mutual understanding.

Mandy slapped the table, distracting them.

With a sigh, Melissa said, "I'd better bathe Mandy and put her down. It's almost her bedtime."

"You run the water and I'll go gather up her diaper and clothes," he said, standing. Mandy snuggled against his chest and laid her head on his shoulder. His heart expanded until he was sure it would burst. "We'd better hurry before she goes to sleep."

Things were working out well, Russ decided as he hurried down the hall with the baby. He and Melissa had more in common than he would have thought.

His smile dimmed, however, when a new thought occurred to him. It wasn't even eight o'clock. What were the two of them going to do after they'd put Mandy to bed?

The idea of spending the rest of the evening alone with Melissa brought some interesting possibilities to mind that made his pulse rate accelerate.

CHAPTER NINE

AFTER MANDY WAS ASLEEP, the awkwardness was even worse than Russ had expected. What was he supposed to do with the rest of the evening? Melissa, too, seemed uneasy.

Finally, she ventured, "I really need to do some paperwork, if—if it won't offend you."

"Offend me?"

"You're my guest. I should—"

"No. Do what you need to do. Are you going to work in your office?" He wanted to protest. He didn't want her to shut herself away from him.

"Actually, I usually work at the kitchen table. My office has gotten too cluttered lately. Do you need anything to eat or drink before I start work?"

"Do you have a sketch pad, a ruler, pencil and eraser?" he asked, suddenly knowing how he wanted to spend his evening.

She supplied him with all he asked for and he sat down across from her at the table. For several hours, they worked together in silence, exchanging smiles occasionally.

When she closed the books she was working on, he laid down his pencil. "Tired?" he asked, wondering how she managed to keep going. Her day had begun with an emotional upset and she hadn't stopped since then.

She smiled and shook her head no. "No more than normal." As she stood, she glanced at the paper he'd been sketching on. "What's that?"

He looked down at the drawing he'd made. "Plans for a house. I've been designing office buildings and work space for so long, I wasn't sure I could still design a house that would be efficient."

"May I see?"

When she bent over his work, he felt a strange tremor of nerves pass through him. He hadn't felt that sensation in a number of years.

"What a lovely home!" she exclaimed, her face beaming. "It's beautiful."

He showed her the intricacies of the design he'd created with all the joy of a proud papa. She asked questions, drawing out his explanation. As they bent over the table, his shoulder brushed against hers and the longing to wrap his arms around her flooded him.

He stepped away, frowning.

"Oh, I'm sorry, I didn't mean to keep you—I'm sure you're tired," she said, unconsciously repeating his earlier words.

"No more than normal," he replied, smiling as he did the same.

"Well—" she drew in a deep breath "—I guess it's time to call it a night. Are you going to build that house?"

"I design office buildings. This house doesn't belong in Chicago. It belongs here, in Wyoming."

"Yes, you're right. I guess maybe someday you'll find a buyer for it."

He shrugged, rolling up the paper as he stood there, waiting for her to move. He was afraid if he moved before she did, he'd take her into his arms.

"I'll say good-night if you don't need anything else." She backed out of the kitchen.

He remained where he was. "Good night."

"Good night," she returned, a soft smile on her lips. Then she ran down the hall.

He dreamed of her all night.

When Russ awoke the next morning, he immediately checked on Mandy. She hadn't yet stirred, so he hurried and dressed for his morning jog, then went to the kitchen to prepare her bottle.

"I'm getting good at this," he muttered to himself. He almost didn't know whether to be horrified or proud at his expertise with a baby.

Leaving the bottle on the kitchen cabinet, he opened Mandy's door again. This time the baby was standing in her bed, holding on to the edge. When she saw Russ, she reached out for him and cooed.

"Sssh, sweetheart," he whispered. "We don't want to wake Mommy."

After changing her diaper and clothes, he carried her to the kitchen to pick up the bottle before settling into the big leather chair in the living room. He and Mandy spent a quiet time while the baby drank her formula.

Melissa's house faced east and sunlight crept in, illuminating the room with a warm glow. The peace of the moment filled him. His mornings in Chicago were rushed, hurried, tense, as was his day at the office.

He could get used to starting his day with Mandy in his arms.

After burping her, he wrapped her in a blanket and strapped her into the umbrella stroller. Then, before they set out for their jog, he carefully wrote a note to Melissa, explaining what he was doing. She'd probably figure it out on her own, but he wasn't taking any chances this morning.

After easing the door shut behind him, Russ took a deep breath, the crisp air filling his lungs.

"Mandy, my girl, are you ready? Hang on tight," he warned, and started down the sidewalk, concentrating on his morning exercise.

Fifteen minutes into his jog, his mind refused to remain on his legs pumping, his muscles heating up. Instead, he thought again of the previous evening. And his pleasure in Melissa's company. He forgot the jogging, the fresh mountain air, the lazy clouds in the sky as he concentrated on Melissa's sweetness.

When he and Mandy turned the corner at the end of the block and slowed to a walk to cool off, Russ was relieved to discover there was no distraught Melissa wondering where her baby could be.

He carried the stroller up the steps and into the house, noting Mandy's closed eyes. He could put her in her bed, but he feared he'd wake her. Deciding to chance it, he pushed her down the hall and into her room. There he unstrapped her and carefully lifted her out of the seat, cuddling her against his chest. Then he laid her down in the bed.

If she stayed asleep, he'd have his shower.

He'd almost made it to the door when she called to him.

"Da-da-da-da."

"Sweetheart, Daddy was going—I mean, *I* was going to take a shower." He walked back to the crib. Russ sighed, wondering how Melissa managed to shower and wash her hair when her daughter demanded so much attention.

Being a parent wasn't as easy as it seemed.

MELISSA TURNED OVER and crossed her arm over her eyes to shut out the light. She didn't want to get up. But, of course, Mandy— Once again she realized Mandy hadn't awakened her before sunrise, as was her usual schedule.

She smiled as she checked her watch. Eight-thirty. Two mornings in a row she'd gotten to sleep late. And this morning, she knew her child had not been kidnapped.

Shoving back the covers, she swung her legs to the floor. She owed Russ Hall a great deal. Today she'd try to repay him by encouraging him to do what he wanted to do, whether it included her or not. He'd earned some freedom.

She stretched, slipped on her robe and headed for the bathroom. The only bathroom. She couldn't help

thinking about the wonderful house Russ had designed last night. Three bathrooms, four bedrooms,
a study, plus a normal living room and family room,
kitchen and dining room.

A sunken tub. The master bath had had a sunken
tub. She could imagine soaking in a real bubble bath,
not the goop from yesterday, luxuriating in peace.

Mandy shrieked.

Melissa smiled. So much for luxuriating in peace.
She washed her face, combed her hair and headed
for the kitchen.

"You're up!" Russ exclaimed. He stood leaning
against the kitchen cabinet, Mandy in his arms, wearing his jogging shorts and nothing else.

She drew a deep breath and averted her eyes. The
man's body was a lethal weapon to a woman's un-
suspecting heart. She couldn't deny the attraction that
filled her every time she got close to him. But it was
physical, nothing else.

"You hungry? Sit down and I'll fix you breakfast," he offered, moving to put Mandy in her high
chair.

"No, I'll fix—"

"You promised to let me help, remember?" he
said, stiffening.

She didn't remember if she'd actually promised
out loud, but she'd certainly vowed to accept his
help. She wanted to make sure she wasn't being a
martyr like her mother.

She reached for Mandy. "Okay, you fix breakfast.
Mandy and I will watch."

He seemed surprised at her acceptance and she almost reassured him that she'd be glad to cook.

"Uh, I don't suppose you could delay eating until after I've grabbed a shower?" he asked, looking embarrassed. "I was afraid to leave Mandy alone after our jog."

"Of course I can wait. I appreciate your taking care of her while I slept in. You've gone way beyond the call of duty. Go take your shower. We'll be right here when you're ready." With breakfast already prepared. And no distracting half-naked man to bother her.

"Oh, I've already fed Mandy her cereal. And I'll hurry."

"Take your time."

She put Mandy in her high chair and cut up pieces of a banana to keep her happy. Then, when she heard the water of the shower running, she began cooking bacon and eggs to go with the muffins she'd prepared last night. By the time Russ appeared in the kitchen doorway, his face clean-shaven, dressed in pressed jeans and shirt, breakfast was on the table.

"Hey, I was going to cook!" he protested.

"I didn't have anything else to do while you were showering," she said. "You wouldn't want me to be bored, would you?"

He grinned. "Okay, you win this round. So lunch is my responsibility."

"Good enough."

He acted as if he'd suddenly remembered something. In the process of sitting down, he froze midway. "And dinner."

"Dinner?" Melissa repeated.

"I'm responsible for dinner, too." He sat down and reached for the salt and pepper, not looking at her.

"It will be my turn for dinner. I'll—"

"Nope. I've already made plans."

"Oh, of course, I didn't realize what you meant. Will you need to borrow the car?" She'd promised herself that Russ would have the day free to do what he wanted. It was ridiculous to be hurt that he'd made plans without her.

"*We'll* need the car."

She frowned. "There aren't too many restaurants that handle children well. Mandy and I will stay home. But you feel free to go where you want."

"I've made plans, and they include you." He gave her a charming smile, as if he knew she'd be pleased.

"Who does 'you' include?"

"Only you. We're not taking Mandy."

Panic filled her. "But I haven't arranged for a sitter."

"I know that. I've learned a lot since I got off that plane. I called Mrs. Tuttle a few minutes ago. She's going to take care of Mandy while we go out to eat." This time his smile was triumphant.

"Oh, no! Mrs. Tuttle gets too tired if she keeps Mandy very long. I don't think—"

"Melissa, parents leave their children with a sitter all the time. There's no reason not to go out for one meal. Mrs. Tuttle said she'd take a nap this afternoon, and I promised we'd be back before ten. It's all settled."

She jumped up. "Don't you think you should've consulted me before you made all these arrangements?"

"No, because you would've argued with me. Just like you're doing now. When's the last time you had a nice dinner out without Mandy?"

Melissa slowly sank into her chair as she frantically tried to remember such an evening. Which was ridiculous because there wasn't one. She'd felt guilty leaving her baby with Mrs. Tuttle while she went to work, much less to play.

"I don't go out often. It's expensive."

"This evening won't cost you a thing. I've already made reservations for seven o'clock. We'll bathe Mandy before we go. All Mrs. Tuttle will have to do is give her a bottle before bedtime."

She could tell by his expression that he expected more protests. She supposed she had been very difficult since his arrival, which didn't make sense since she'd invited him into her house so he could help her.

But all she'd really intended was to sleep late on Mother's Day. Instead, Russ Hall had taken care of Mandy for two mornings. She owed him her cooperation. She almost chuckled out loud. Her thought sounded so self-sacrificing. Dinner out with a handsome man was definitely not a sacrifice.

"Thank you. That's very thoughtful of you,

Russ," she said, and picked up her fork to eat her breakfast.

Though she didn't look at him, she could feel his gaze on her, but she chewed as normally as possible, pretending that his invitation was a common occurrence. Much to her relief, he finally began eating, also.

Once breakfast was finished, he joined her at the sink, helping with the dishes. She graciously thanked him and handed him a towel.

In no time, that task was completed.

"Now what?" he asked.

"I don't know. I don't have any more chores to do right now. I'm sorry to disappoint you since I know you love to do them." She gave him a cheeky grin.

His hand came up to hold her chin. "Watch it, lady, or I'll grab a mop and start on the floors."

She immediately rose to the bait. "I mopped my floors on Thursday!" His chuckle had her adding, "But, of course, I'd be delighted for you to clean them again. Shall I bring you the mop?"

He dropped a kiss on her upturned mouth, then crossed the room to the high chair. "I think I'd better use my cleaning expertise on little Miss Mandy instead. Otherwise, she won't be fit to go to the mall with us."

Melissa decided Russ must be in the habit of dishing out casual kisses. If she made a big deal about it, he'd know how much his touch disturbed her. "Uh, we're going to the mall?"

"Yeah, if you don't mind. I want to buy Mandy a teddy bear. She doesn't have one, does she?"

"No, but you don't need to buy her presents."

"I know I don't need to. I want to. You're not going to fuss about that, too, are you?"

"No, of course not," she replied. "But Mandy has a lot of toys."

"Yeah, but I want to give her something to remember me by. Every kid should have a teddy bear."

"Did you have one?"

She should have known better. Any question about his childhood sent him in retreat.

"Yes," he said abruptly, then crossed to the sink to wet a paper towel before returning to wipe Mandy's face and hands. "Does she need to change clothes before we go?"

"Yes."

"You pick something out for her to wear and I'll dress her while you get ready."

She looked down, having forgotten she was still in her robe and nightgown. How strange that she could be so casual around a man she barely knew.

Hurrying out of the kitchen, she called over her shoulder, "Thanks, I'll do that."

She really was getting the hang of letting Russ help her out.

AN HOUR LATER, Russ pushed Mandy's stroller through the mall, feeling like the daddy he was pretending to be.

"Lots of babies here today," he whispered to Melissa, who was walking beside him.

"That's because it's the weekend. During the week, the mall is almost empty."

She smiled at him and he gripped the stroller handles to keep from reaching for her. He'd already overstepped the boundaries with that kiss in the kitchen. But, hell, she was tough to resist.

"Uh, where's a toy store?"

"The toy store is at the other end of the mall, but you'll probably find more teddy bears at a baby store. If that's still what you're looking for."

He raised one eyebrow. There seemed to be a question somewhere in her words, but he wasn't sure what it was. "Yeah, that's what I'm looking for."

She guided him to a shop nearby, its windows filled with tiny clothes, several elaborate cribs and stuffed animals. One particular bear caught his eye. It wasn't huge, like the white bear in the corner. It was brown, much the color of a real bear, with a lovable face. Black eyes and a big black nose were embroidered on its face.

"I like that one," he suggested, pointing out the brown bear.

Melissa seemed relieved. "That one is perfect. It's just the size Mandy will enjoy. I was afraid you were going to go for one of those giant things."

"I considered it," he told her with a grin. "Let's see if Mandy likes my choice."

When the saleslady got the bear out of the window, since it was the last they had in that style, Russ knelt in front of the stroller and held the bear in front of Mandy.

"Da-da-da-da!" the baby exclaimed, reaching for the bear.

"I think she likes it," Russ told Melissa, grinning. "And it's soft enough. Feel."

Melissa touched the bear and assured him his choice was great.

"We'll take it," he told the saleslady. "May I cut the tag off so she can play with it?"

The woman took a pair of scissors and snipped the tag free, then handed the bear back to Russ. He knelt in front of Mandy again and offered it to her. She grabbed the bear and immediately carried it to her mouth.

"Is she trying to eat it or kiss it?" Russ asked, watching in fascination.

"Probably both. I'm not sure she can differentiate between the two at this point."

He pulled his wallet out of his pocket and handed the saleslady his charge card.

"Will there be anything else, sir? We've got a special on summer play clothes. Your daughter would look cute in that pink outfit," she said, gesturing to a plastic model wearing a pink T-shirt with stars on it, accompanied by a pair of pink shorts.

"Hey, I like that. What size does Mandy wear?" he asked Melissa.

"Russ, you've already bought her a toy. That's really all—"

"Come on, Melissa, let me have some fun."

"Fine," she agreed reluctantly. "One outfit."

He grinned. "And maybe some sandals. She'll need sandals with those shorts."

Fifteen minutes later, thoroughly enjoying himself, he'd amassed a pile of purchases for Mandy. He gathered up all their bags, leaving Melissa to push the stroller as they left the store. Mandy, chewing on her teddy bear's ear, was content.

"Time for lunch." He'd had a big breakfast, thanks to Melissa, but it was almost two o'clock.

She checked her watch. "Oh, the pictures will be ready in five minutes. Could we swing by there and pick them up? I'm anxious to see how they turned out."

"Sure. I'll go pick up the car first. It should be ready by now." They had left the car at a garage across from the mall to have the tire repaired. "Is there a restaurant near the photo place?"

"Are you in the mood for Mexican? Dos Hombres is right across from it."

"Sounds good. And we can stow all our packages in the car." As they walked toward the mall exit, he added, "I may have gotten a little carried away, but I had fun."

"I'm glad, because I won't need to buy Mandy anything for months. Even then, she'll still be able to wear the blue jeans."

"They're cute, aren't they? She'll need them if I put her on a horse again. She's got to look the part. Maybe I should buy her a hat."

"No! No more purchases for Mandy. Besides, you

won't be around to take her riding, remember? You'll be back in Chicago.''

Her words hit him hard. He'd been pretending Melissa and her baby had a permanent place in his life. But he wouldn't see them after this weekend.

Unless he came back for a visit. Or moved back to Wyoming—a possibility he'd promised himself he'd consider.

He hadn't been back to Wyoming once in the fourteen years he'd been gone. But now he was contemplating a return trip in a month or two.

And maybe another at Christmas. He'd have to see Mandy at Christmastime. He could go to FAO Schwartz in Chicago to find her a great Christmas present. And deliver it personally.

What would he bring Melissa?

An immediate vision of something out of Victoria's Secret formed in his mind. Dangerous thought. He shook his head to clear it and realized Melissa had stopped a few feet back, staring at a tuxedo rental shop.

"Melissa?"

"Oh, sorry. I just—Russ, would you consider posing for a few more pictures?"

"Sure, if you want me to. What do you have in mind?"

"I was thinking—you'll think I'm crazy, but the contrast of you in a tuxedo against a rugged backdrop, you know, civilization against the wilderness... I think it would be great. We can rent you a tuxedo and—"

"No need. I brought my own. Getting a tuxedo to fit me isn't easy, and I didn't know what you had in mind, so I came prepared."

She smiled radiantly at him, making him glad he'd bothered. Anything that made Melissa happy was a good thing.

"That's perfect!"

He grinned back. "Do we get to eat lunch first?"

"Of course. I'll need to go back and get my equipment after we eat. Then I know the perfect place. There's a bluff that looks down on the Platte River. You'll love it."

Somehow, he was sure she was right.

CHAPTER TEN

RUSS ORDERED A PLATE of nachos to eat while they waited for their meal. Then he looked at Melissa.

"Okay, how did they turn out?"

While he'd driven them to the restaurant, she'd taken a quick peek at the pictures, but he hadn't seen any of them.

From the look on his face, she thought he might be nervous, which was ridiculous.

"I think I'm going to have to pay you a modeling fee." In fact, from the glimpse she'd taken, she was convinced Russ would make her rich. She pulled the first set of pictures from the envelope. Making sure the table had no moisture on it, she began laying out the proofs of the photos they'd taken in the barn.

"You're a good photographer," Russ commented as he studied himself.

"I had great material to work with." She stacked those photos and slid them back into the envelope.

The next group included Russ leaning against the stall with the horse nuzzling his shoulder. "Oh, Russ, look," she said with a smile. "The horse is as good a model as you."

"But I'm more handsome, aren't I?" he teased.

"Definitely." She hoped the man didn't know how much she was bowled over by his attractiveness.

When they got to the pictures in the bubble bath, Russ was actually embarrassed at the sexiness of his image.

"Well, you were right about the contrast, all right, but I don't think anyone will want a picture of me in a bathtub." He frowned as he continued to study the photos.

Melissa chuckled. "I think these will sell out the minute they go on the market." One photo in particular, where he was wearing his cocky grin, his hat tilted down, his arms resting on the edge of the tub, was worth the entire day's shoot. "I think I'll give this one to the reporter coming tomorrow."

"What reporter?" he asked with a frown.

"Don't you remember? The local paper promised to do a follow-up on each bachelor's weekend. I scheduled an interview for tomorrow afternoon."

"I don't want to do an interview," he protested, still frowning.

"But that was the whole point to my bidding on a bachelor at the auction. To use him as a model, then have it promoted in the media."

"But everyone will know who I am when they buy that card with me sitting in a tub as if I were naked!"

"You're wearing your swimsuit."

"I wanted to—you seemed—" He paused and drew a deep breath. "Okay. Okay, I'll do the interview. Probably no one will remember my name, anyway."

Only every woman in Wyoming. "Mostly I sell to tourists. They'll never see the article."

"Good."

The waitress appeared beside their table with the nachos, and Melissa hurriedly began scooping up the pictures.

"Wow! Those are some pictures!" the woman exclaimed, staring at Russ and then the photos.

"Yes, they are, aren't they?" Melissa replied, pleased at the waitress's reaction. She could do a line of note cards, too. Maybe even a calendar. Wrapped up in her thoughts, she scarcely noticed when the woman finally served the nachos and left.

"Melissa?" Russ said. "What are you thinking about?"

"My business. Russ, I think I really do need to pay you for your work."

"Nope. I agreed to it. You bought my services for the weekend, remember?"

"Yes, but—"

"No argument. Let's relax before we start working again."

IT WAS DEFINITELY WORK. Russ wasn't naive enough to think modeling was fun, but he hadn't realized just how much work was involved.

Mandy was sitting in her stroller, holding her bear, while he posed in front of a cliff on the banks of the Platte River. He was wearing his tuxedo and Sam's cowboy hat again. Along with his own boots. Fortunately they were black.

"Okay. Take off your hat and hold it in front of you."

"Why?"

"Because you have good hair, and it's a pose all the cowboys make in westerns." She smiled at him. "Pretend you've come calling on the schoolmarm."

He shook his head but did as she asked. It wasn't hard to pretend. After all, if Melissa were the schoolmarm, he'd definitely come calling.

"Wonderful," she muttered as she moved around him. Then she paused. "Um, Russ, is there any chance you could look shy?"

"Shy?"

"You needn't make it sound like a foreign word, mister," she teased. "Surely you didn't leave the cradle with that knowing grin."

No, he hadn't left the cradle believing he'd held the world in his hands. In fact, when he'd first come to the ranch, he hadn't spoken for almost a month. Mrs. Duncan had once told him she'd feared he would never talk again.

It had taken him a long time to shed his vulnerability. Or at least hide it.

He lowered his chin and gave a half smile, his hat in his hand. After Melissa snapped a number of pictures, he raised his eyebrows. "Don't you think you've taken enough shots? You've already got at least a hundred from yesterday."

"Are you too tired?"

"Hell, no, I'm not too tired. But how many pictures do you need of one guy in a tuxedo?"

Mandy protested, as if she, too, wanted an answer to that question. Melissa put down her camera and dug into the diaper bag for a teething biscuit for her daughter. "I'll trade you the biscuit for the bear, sweetie."

Reluctantly, Mandy made the trade, but she watched her mother until the bear disappeared in the diaper bag, as if she wanted to know where to find her toy.

Melissa then turned her attention to Russ. Walking over, she said, "Just a few more pictures, please?"

His voice was gruff when he agreed, because he didn't want her to know how easily she could gain his cooperation. Whatever she asked for would immediately be hers if he had any say in the matter.

She reached up to touch his bow tie. "May I undo this? We want a relaxed look, as if you've just come in from a great night."

He stood still as a statue as she undid his tie, then took out the first two studs, spreading the lapels of his shirt slightly.

"Mmm, nice," she said under her breath.

Nice? He'd wanted her to continue to undress him until he was free of the monkey suit and could return the favor. And make love with her in the waning sunlight.

"I've noticed you tend to undress me every time you get a chance," he teased to distract himself, loving the way her cheeks heated up.

In spite of her embarrassment, she grinned at him. "It's a female thing. You wouldn't understand."

"Oh, I think I might," he muttered, hoping she couldn't read his mind.

Mandy shrieked and he was reminded of her presence. How did married couples ever manage any time alone? Mandy had napped through most of lunch. Did parents have to plan their sex life around a baby's naptime? Or were they always limited to nighttime activities, when they were both exhausted?

"What are you thinking about?" Melissa asked, curiosity in her voice.

Russ could feel his own cheeks flushing. "Nothing! I mean—I don't know. Why?"

"You seemed very intent on something."

Oh, yeah. He'd been intent, all right. In fact, it was fortunate she'd interrupted him, because his body had begun to respond to the thought of making love to Melissa. He didn't want that in the pictures.

THEY GOT HOME LATER than Russ had intended. It was almost six-thirty and their reservations were for seven.

"We're going to have to hurry," he said as he carried Mandy into the house. "Shall we bathe Mandy first?"

"No, I have to feed her some dinner first. Why don't you get ready while I do that."

"But you won't have much time to get ready."

"I'm used to working around Mandy's schedule. Just go get ready."

He grabbed a quick shower and dressed in navy

slacks, a long-sleeved pale blue shirt, a red-and-blue-striped tie and a navy blazer.

Melissa had Mandy in the sink, bathing her, when he made it back to the kitchen.

"You go dress and I'll finish up with Mandy," he said.

"She's bathed already. I'll dry her off and let you diaper and dress her. If you take her now, you'll have water all over you."

She was right, but the evening wasn't starting out the way he'd planned.

He'd just finished dressing Mandy when the doorbell rang. "I'll get it," he called so Melissa wouldn't worry. Swinging open the door, he discovered Mrs. Tuttle, as he'd expected.

"Come in, Mrs. Tuttle. You're right on time."

"Yes. My, you look fine, Russ. I'm so glad you had this idea. Melissa deserves a special evening."

Well, at least they were in agreement there. "Thanks for your help, Mrs. Tuttle. We've bathed Mandy and fed her dinner. About eight, she takes her bottle. Then Melissa puts her in bed and winds up the music box on her mobile."

"My, you are good with babies, aren't you? Most men don't know what to do with them."

Russ almost laughed aloud. Two nights ago, he would have sworn he'd never know a thing about babies. Now Mrs. Tuttle thought he was an expert. "Thanks. Mandy's an easy baby, or else Melissa's a good teacher."

Before the elderly lady could reply, Melissa spoke

from behind him. "I hope you don't mind baby-sitting, Mrs. Tuttle."

Russ turned around and almost swallowed his tongue. Melissa was wearing a black dress that faithfully followed the curves of her body, inviting a man's hands to do likewise. While the neckline was modest, the hemline was high, drawing attention to her long legs.

He whistled. "Quite a change, Melissa."

She shrugged her shoulders, but he could tell his enthusiasm had embarrassed her. "Better than jeans?"

"Oh, yeah."

"Now, you two run along. Me and Mandy are going to watch television and play before bedtime." Mrs. Tuttle beamed at them, as if they'd been particularly good children. But Russ wasn't feeling like a little boy. And he didn't think Melissa looked like an innocent.

He put his hand on her back to urge her to the door and came to an abrupt halt when his palm met only warm, silky skin.

"Mmm, nice dress," he mumbled, licking his lips. The modest neckline flowed into a cowl at the back that dipped almost to her waist, baring her back.

"Thank you," she said, hurrying to the door as if avoiding his touch.

He hoped the restaurant had dancing. He sure as hell was going to be looking for another excuse to put his hands on her tonight. Just following her out the door, his gaze glued to her soft skin, had him itching to pull her against him.

He cleared his throat after getting in the car. "I wasn't sure you'd have anything to wear since you'd said you don't date."

She gave a nervous laugh. "I wasn't sure I would have, either. I—I haven't worn this dress since before Mandy was born. I wasn't sure it would fit."

"Oh, yeah, it fits. It fits so well I'm not sure I should let you out in public."

She sent him an alarmed look. "Do you mean it's too tight?"

Russ started the car and began backing out of the driveway. "No, it's not too tight. Every man in Casper would vote that it's perfect, Melissa. But I'm not sure I want them all admiring your—you. I may have to fight them off when they get a look at you."

"You're being silly," she protested, a breathless quality in her voice that made him want to seal her lips with his.

Man, he was in trouble.

MELISSA KNEW THE EVENING was a bad idea. She'd realized how dangerous it was going to be when she'd put on her black dress. It made her feel...sexy. Which went along with the way Russ made her feel.

She was a mother. She didn't need to feel sexy. There was no time in her life for a man.

There was no room for romance.

Glancing up from the candle in the center of the table, she studied Russ's face across from her.

Whether there was room or not, romance was here. Right here in Casper, Wyoming. Right here in Russ's gaze.

"You're not eating. Is something wrong with your steak?" Russ asked, leaning forward.

"No, but I—I've lost my appetite."

"Maybe a little exercise will help. Let's dance."

The restaurant had a small dance floor, and a four-piece band was playing soft music. Melissa felt her pulse quicken at the thought of moving into Russ's embrace.

"Oh, I'm not a good dancer. I'd step on your toes." Or melt all over him.

"No problem," he assured her as he stood, holding out a hand.

"Really, Russ, I'm a horrible dancer."

He didn't sit back down. Instead, he picked up her hand and tugged gently. "Come on, sweetheart. I don't think I can concentrate on my steak until we get past this dance. Obviously, you can't, either."

She was surprised that he would admit a vulnerability to her. "You aren't hungry?"

"Oh, I'm hungry. But not for steak."

He tugged again and she stood. Leading her the short distance to the dance floor, he wrapped both arms around her and pulled her completely into his embrace. What movement he made in time to the slow music was minimal.

"Uhm, Russ," she muttered, "I think we're supposed to move."

"We're doing just fine. This dress is killing me."

She leaned back and stared at him. "What do you mean?"

"It lets me touch your skin. And makes me want to touch more."

She gulped and buried her nose against his throat. This wasn't a conversation she wanted to have. But as his hands slid across her back, she understood what he meant. She wanted to feel his hands all over her body.

But it was a physical response. That was all.

She wasn't used to lying to herself. It made her uncomfortable. The truth was, Russ Hall was getting to her. She'd isolated herself from the male half of the population since Greg's death. And, of course, she had no social life.

It was she and Mandy against the world. With a little help from Mrs. Tuttle.

Then Russ Hall arrived on her doorstep. She'd thought she could invite him into her house and remain distant. Foolish woman.

He stirred longings in her she thought she'd dismissed from her life. Not just physical ones. The sharing of both good times and bad. The comfort of another adult to rely on. The warmth and caring of a man who'd been a stranger two days ago.

And then there was the physical need. The growing hunger to be touched by this man, to share physical intimacy again. To believe that she was beautiful in his eyes. Who cared what the rest of the world thought as long as he—

"I can't do this," she whispered, and broke from

his arms. She heard his footsteps as he followed her to the table, but she didn't turn around.

When she was seated at the table again, she had no choice but to face him.

"What happened?" he asked, his voice husky.

Gazing into Russ's eyes was difficult, but she wasn't going to play coy or pretend she didn't know what was wrong. Lifting her chin, she said, "I'm attracted to you, Russ. It's a physical reaction I don't seem able to control, and it complicates my life in a way I don't want."

He said nothing but continued to stare at her.

"It's my fault," she continued. "This entire weekend was an ill-conceived idea. I didn't consider the human aspect of my plan. But we both know it ends tomorrow. You return to your life in Chicago. I stay here with Mandy. We never see each other again. So we need to keep things simple."

"How do we do that?" he asked quietly.

For a second she saw something in his gaze that had her heart racing. But she dismissed it as fantasy on her part. "We stop touching. We eat our meal and go home and pretend that nothing happened."

One corner of his mouth, that firm, delicious mouth, slid upward. "I don't know if I can pretend that well."

Without his help, she didn't know if she could, either. "You have to, Russ. For Mandy's sake."

"Mandy?"

"I want to be a good mother. I want Mandy to have a happy life." She wasn't explaining this right.

It sounded selfish to tell him how miserable she'd be when he got on that plane. It was ridiculous to complain that he'd awakened her from her trance, from her self-induced sleep. It was absurd to blame him for her weakness.

She tried to smile but felt her lips tremble. "I'm not explaining this the way I meant to. But what—what we're experiencing is physical. It will go away...unless we carry it any further. And I don't want to.

HE'D NEVER FORCED a woman in his life. He certainly wouldn't, couldn't, force Melissa. But damn, he wanted her, more than he'd wanted any woman in his life.

But she was right. Melissa didn't come alone. Sweet Mandy was involved. So there would be no sharing of a bed in her little house tonight. There would be no relief to the raging hunger that threatened to overpower his good sense.

"Then I guess that settles everything. Finish your steak and we'll go. Mrs. Tuttle will be surprised when we show up early."

"I'm sorry, Russ. I didn't intend—"

"To seduce me? Don't worry about it. I shouldn't be so easily tempted. But, just for the record, Melissa, you're a beautiful, sensual woman. And I want you."

The color in her cheeks rose and she stared at her plate.

"But you're right. You deserve more than a one-night fling. But don't shut yourself away. Don't stop living. Mandy…Mandy needs you to do that.''

She lifted her eyes and met his gaze head-on. ''I will always be there for my child. I love her with all my heart.''

''I know.''

They both tried to finish their meal with no further conversation. Russ found the succulent steak flavorless. All he could think about was that even though Melissa sat across from him, she might as well have been on the other side of the Rockies.

Finally he signaled the waiter, asking for to-go boxes and the check. When the man hurried away, he looked at Melissa. ''Is that all right with you?''

''Yes, please,'' she said.

''Not exactly what I had in mind when I planned our dinner. I wanted you to have a good time.'' Was he being honest with himself? Had he been thinking of her? Or had he wanted to get her to himself, without even baby Mandy to chaperone them?

''It was thoughtful, but I think it best we call it an evening.''

He paid the bill, then escorted her from the restaurant. The Wyoming sky, clear of clouds this evening, blazed with a million stars in all their glory. Even in Casper, the air was clear, energizing.

Without thinking, he put his hand on her back to guide her. When his fingertips touched her warm skin, he jerked them back as if he'd touched a live wire. ''Sorry,'' he muttered, and gestured to where he'd parked her car.

She ducked her head and hurried forward.

"There are a lot of stars out tonight," he said, hoping to distract her from his mistake.

"Yes."

"Maybe we'll see a falling star. Want to make a wish?" He'd seen a few out on the ranch, away from the city lights. He'd even made a few wishes before he'd grown too old to believe in them anymore.

"Yes, I'd like to make a wish."

"What would it be?"

In the dim light from the restaurant, she turned to look at him, and he held his breath at the sadness in her gaze. "If I tell, it won't come true."

He had a sinking suspicion that she was wishing him back in Chicago, where he wouldn't upset her carefully ordered life.

But that wouldn't be his wish.

CHAPTER ELEVEN

HIS LAST MORNING IN CASPER.

Today Russ changed his routine. No morning jog. He had other things to do. The first was tend to Mandy so Melissa could have another sleep-in.

He quietly opened the door to Melissa's study and stared at the figure sprawled on the sofa. Then he tiptoed into the room, his gaze searching. When he saw the illuminated dial of an alarm clock on the floor by the sofa, he knew his suspicions had been on target. She'd set an alarm so she wouldn't sleep in this morning.

Mother's Day, and she intended to get up.

Without bothering to turn off the alarm, he followed the cord to the wall and unplugged the clock. With a grim smile of satisfaction, he crossed to the door. Before he stepped through it, he turned for one more look at the sleeping beauty.

Then he closed the door behind him.

Just as he would close this episode in his life. After all, a woman and her baby had no place in his life. His response to Melissa was physical. That was what she had said last night. And he agreed.

Next he entered Mandy's room. He crossed to the

bed to discover the baby girl lying there, drowsily staring at the mobile above her head.

"Hey there, sweetheart. Ready to get up?"

As if she understood his words, she rolled to her side and sat up before she pulled herself to a standing position, her smile bright.

"You know," he whispered, picking her up, "it amazes me that your mommy could have a baby who's such a morning person. You and I have a lot in common."

Once he'd changed and diapered the baby, the two of them were seated in the leather chair, peacefully greeting the sun.

"I wasn't thinking yesterday," he explained to his earnest audience. "I should have found a present for your mommy. After all, it's Mother's Day. You should give her something. So, when you finish your bottle, we're going to go find a gift for her."

He wasn't sure what he could find at six on a Sunday morning, but they'd come up with something.

Half an hour later, he and Mandy stood in the entrance of a convenience store, staring at their choices. He rubbed the back of his neck in frustration as he held Mandy against him. "I don't know, Mandy, my girl, beef jerky just doesn't seem festive."

She babbled something in return, but he didn't find her contribution helpful.

"May I help you, sir?" the woman behind the counter called out.

He shrugged as he approached her. "Well, you

see, I forgot it was Mother's Day until this morning. We're looking for a present. You seem to be the only store open.''

She grinned. "Just like a man."

"Ouch. Do you think she'll forgive me?"

"Where is she now?"

"Home in bed. We're letting her sleep in, aren't we, Mandy?"

The woman sighed. "She'll forgive you. If my husband, ex-husband, that is, had ever thought of letting me sleep in, I would've even put up with his—" her gaze flew to Mandy "—his shenanigans."

"Thanks," Russ muttered, appreciating her amending her words, even if Mandy wouldn't understand what she meant.

"Here's what I've got. There are some cut flowers for sale at the end of that aisle. Those always go over big. Then on the aisle against the cooler, I've got a few bottles of nail polish, some remover, nail files, that kind of thing. It's about all I have to offer, unless she'd like some potato chips or a hot dog."

Russ smiled. "Those are good ideas, thanks." Carrying Mandy, he found the nail polish. There were six colors. The green and blue he immediately decided against. He didn't think Melissa would like those colors. The other four were various shades of pink.

"What do you think, Mandy?" he asked, holding the four small bottles in his hand.

Mandy reached for one of them and took it straight to her mouth.

"No, sweetheart, don't eat it!" he exclaimed. In reaching for that bottle, he managed to drop the other three. Great. That's all he needed, to spill nail polish over the floor.

Fortunately, none of the bottles broke. He gathered them up. "Tell you what, Mandy, why don't we splurge and buy all four. Then Mommy can decide which one she likes best." The woman had mentioned some other things. He scoured the shelf, finding a nail file, some clippers and a bottle of hand lotion.

"She won't mistake this for a gift from Neiman Marcus, but at least our hearts are in the right place. Now, let's find those flowers and we're out of here," he assured his companion, who kept trying to grab the nail polish again.

He carried his purchases to the counter, then went to the end of the nearest aisle to pick out a bouquet of flowers wrapped in plastic. They looked a little limp, but they were better than nothing.

The clerk beamed at him. "You're really getting into the spirit of the day, young man. I bet your wife will be really pleased."

"Thanks. You wouldn't happen to have any kind of box, would you?"

"Hmm, well, I have this box the packages of bubble gum came in. I mean, it ain't festive, but it is a box."

Russ chuckled. He sure hoped Melissa had a sense of humor when she woke up this morning. The lame excuses for presents wouldn't impress any woman he knew, especially wrapped in a bubble gum box. "I'll take it. And thanks for your help."

He also bought a half dozen doughnuts.

When he and Mandy reached home, the house was still silent. He put Mandy in her playpen and found some of the paper he'd used two nights ago when he drew the house plans. Carefully, he cut a piece of paper in half, folded it, then drew some flowers on the face of it.

"This is crazy, making a card like this for a lady who has her own card company. You'll do a better job when you're older, Mandy. But I'm doing the best I can right now."

Inside, he finally wrote, after long consideration, "Thanks for being a great mom. Love, Mandy." Then he put the note and his purchases, except for the flowers, in the bubble gum box.

After opening most of the cabinets in the kitchen, he found a vase for the flowers. He added water and the flowers and set the vase in the middle of the table.

He put the bubble gum box at the place where Melissa usually sat, then he returned to the living room. Mandy was playing with her teddy bear, a happy smile on her face.

Picking up the paper he'd brought in from the front porch, he settled in the leather chair and read the news of the day, hoping he hadn't made a fool of himself with his efforts.

MELISSA ROLLED OVER and stretched, pulling the cover with her. She needed to get up, but she was enjoying the sleep so much. Three days in a row—

She'd set the alarm! Grabbing the clock, she stared at it, noting how dark the dial was. Had the electricity gone off? Then she discovered the clock had been unplugged.

Had she done that in her sleep?

"No!" That was a ridiculous thought. The only person who could have unplugged her clock was Russ Hall. Uneasiness filled her at the thought of him coming in while she was sleeping.

She grabbed her robe and slipped down the hall to the bathroom. She refused to face the man without combing her hair and washing her face.

Even if he meant nothing to her. Absolutely nothing.

She found both Russ and Mandy in the living room. Mandy squealed when she saw her mother, dropping her teddy bear to pull herself to her feet.

"Ma-ma-ma-ma!"

"Hi, baby," she said softly as Russ's face appeared from behind the newspaper.

He folded it and stood, scooping up Mandy from her playpen. "I didn't realize you'd awakened."

"I would've gotten up sooner, but something happened to my alarm clock." She couldn't help smiling at him.

"I'm sorry. I didn't know you wanted to get up early today. I thought the whole point to my coming was so you could sleep late this morning. It's

Mother's Day, you know." He offered her a charming smile.

Her smile turned rueful as she thanked him. "I feel like I've taken advantage of you again." Then their discussion of yesterday, when he'd kissed her, came to mind, and she turned a bright red. Especially when she looked up and found his gaze focused on her lips.

They both abruptly moved at the same time and bumped into each other.

"Oops, sorry. Right, Mandy? We didn't mean to knock Mommy over. Sit down, Melissa. I'll pour you some coffee."

She wasn't going to argue with him about the coffee. She needed it too much. Then she stopped. "Where did those flowers come from?"

"Mandy and I bought them. But not from a florist. I forgot until this morning. Sorry, they're not the best but—"

"Don't you dare apologize." Tears filled her eyes. He'd bought her flowers for Mother's Day. She couldn't believe such thoughtfulness.

"Oh, boy," he muttered. "If you don't like the flowers, you're going to hate the rest."

"What are you talking about? Of course I love them."

He put Mandy in her high chair. Then he turned back to Melissa. "Uh, Mandy and I got a late start on shopping."

"Shopping for what?" Her legs were trembling,

so she sank down into her chair, hoping he wouldn't notice.

"A Mother's Day present."

She covered her eyes with both hands. "No, you weren't supposed to—that's not necessary."

He crossed over to the counter and poured her a cup of coffee. "Here. You'd better take a drink." Then he sat down across from her.

She took a sip of hot coffee, grateful for the caffeine kick. She needed it.

He nudged a box toward her.

She stared at it. Bubble gum? She looked at him.

"The convenience store was the only thing open. I didn't think you'd want chips and dip, or beef jerky. Mandy and I got you the best we could. It's not much."

Those tears that had filled her eyes wouldn't stay there. She stared at the man across from her as they ran down her cheeks. "You actually bought me a Mother's Day present?"

"Mandy and I did. She helped pick it out, didn't you, sweetheart," he said, looking at the baby for confirmation.

Mandy waved at him and gurgled.

"Don't go all mushy on me, Melissa. You'd better open it first."

She lifted off the lid and stared at what was inside.

She'd intended to be distant, polite this morning. To graciously thank him for his assistance. To promise to send him a copy of the cards she made from the photos. To tell him to have a nice trip back.

To get him the hell out of her house before she made a fool of herself.

Too late.

"Oh, Russ, this is so sweet," she whispered, gently touching each item in the box. Then she picked up the paper folded in the middle. When she opened it and read the message, her heart overflowed.

"It's not much. I mean, I know it can't compare to the cards you make, but like I said, we were desperate."

"I—I can't tell you how much this means to me. I won't ever forget my—my first Mother's Day." She leaped to her feet, bent down to kiss Mandy and stared at Russ. But she couldn't say any more. Without another word, she ran from the room.

HALF AN HOUR LATER, Melissa reappeared in the living room. She was firmly in control, having showered and dressed.

Russ watched her warily as she came to a halt near the door to the kitchen. "Thank you again for the present."

"It was nothing," he assured her. In fact, it had done the opposite of what he wanted. It had made her cry.

"I think I'll have some more coffee now, and maybe a doughnut or two. Would you like more coffee?" She seemed poised for flight, waiting for his answer.

"Yeah, but I can get it."

"No! I'll bring it to you. Would you like some bacon and eggs?"

"No, I snitched a couple of your doughnuts. But thank you." If they got any more polite, she'd put on white gloves and he'd don a top hat. This was ridiculous.

She brought him a fresh cup of coffee and set it on the lamp table, staying as far from him as possible. She wasn't wearing a sexy dress today, but he still wanted to touch her. To hold her.

Obviously, she wasn't interested.

"I'll see if Mandy needs a change," she said, not looking at him as she picked up the baby and left the room.

He sat in the chair, waiting for her return, wondering what he should do. She was clearly uncomfortable around him. Hell, he'd been on his best behavior last night. He hadn't hauled her into his arms and carried her down the hall to her bed. He'd politely escorted her home, then walked Mrs. Tuttle to her door. When he'd returned, Melissa had been in the study with the door closed.

At nine o'clock.

And even though he'd stayed up late, watching an old movie on the television, she hadn't come out of her temporary bedroom.

Melissa came back down the hall, Mandy held in front of her, as if she was a barrier to keep Russ away.

"I think Mandy might take a short nap. If you

want to take the car and—and visit old haunts or whatever, feel free to do so.''

"No, thanks. We'll wait until she wakes up, then go out to lunch."

"There's no need. I can fix—"

"It's Mother's Day, Melissa. I'm not going to let you fix a meal."

"What's the big deal?" she asked, a tight smile on her face. "When you first got here, you hardly knew it was Mother's Day."

He set his coffee cup down and stood. "When I first got here, I didn't know how hard it is to be a mother. I didn't know you were a terrific mother. I didn't know I was going to love Mandy." He bit his tongue before he could go too far. "We're going out to eat and I don't want any argument."

"I don't have anything else to wear." She looked at him as if her lack of wardrobe would convince him to change his plans.

"I was going to suggest that barbecue place again, Roy's. You're dressed perfectly for that."

"Fine. We'll go eat barbecue, but we have to be back here by one-thirty. The reporter is coming at two." She turned on her heel and carried Mandy out of the room.

"Damn!" He'd forgotten all about the reporter. She intended to give him the bathtub picture to print in the paper. With a sigh, he realized he'd be gone before it came out. That was some compensation, he guessed.

His plane left at six.

When he'd arrived on Thursday evening, he'd figured the weekend was going to be one of the longest of his life. Even then, he'd been looking forward to his return flight.

Now he didn't know what he wanted.

Melissa came back into the room. "We're ready."

"I thought Mandy was going to take a nap."

"She's not sleepy," Melissa assured him, not meeting his gaze.

So she'd made up the nap to try to get rid of him. He rubbed his chin, then remembered he hadn't shaved. "I'll need a couple of minutes," he said.

"Fine. Take your time. We're in no hurry, as long as we get back by one-thirty."

Yeah. The publicity. He got the picture. This was going to be one hell of a day. He strode down the hall, irritation filling him.

An hour later, he was just as irritated. Melissa hadn't relaxed the entire meal. She'd answered any questions he'd asked in as few words as possible. After staring out the window while he got their food, she'd scarcely looked up.

Mandy, on the other hand, was having a great time. After feeding her some baby food, Melissa had taken one of the rolls and broken it into tiny pieces for the baby.

"I think Mandy likes the bread," he finally commented.

"Yes."

"Want some more iced tea?"

"No, thank you."

"Aha!" he exclaimed, catching her attention. "You actually used three words to answer me. That must be a record."

Her cheeks turned bright red, and he regretted teasing her. "I'm sorry. I have a headache."

"Sweetheart, I'm sorry about the lousy presents this morning. I should've done better."

Her eyes widened and she stared at him. "You think I'm upset about the gift?"

"It seemed the safest possibility. You've hardly spoken to me since you got up."

She bent her head, and he figured she wouldn't answer. But he was wrong. Her honesty last night had surprised him. But apparently it was a character trait.

"I'm embarrassed. I didn't expect you to—you surprised me, and I—I don't like to cry in front of people."

"You're treating me like a low-down, ornery polecat because you're embarrassed?" He smiled, letting her know he was teasing her. He was pretty sure why she was acting so distant this morning. It had a lot to do with last night.

She nodded.

He reached for her hand, but she hurriedly tucked it under the table. "I thought you were angry that I didn't get you a better present."

She shook her head. "I'll always treasure my first Mother's Day gift," she whispered.

He remained silent, watching her, wondering what else he could do to put her at ease. His gaze fell on her almost-full plate. "Do you think you could eat a little, now that we've cleared up that misunderstanding?"

Like an obedient child, she took a bite of barbecue and chewed, staring at her plate.

He sighed. It was a start. Maybe by the time they got home, she'd be treating him like a friend again.

When two o'clock rolled around, he hadn't made a lot of progress. He was sure now her behavior was as much about last night as it was about her embarrassment over her tears. He didn't think she was ready to accept any kind of relationship, even friendship, with another man. Yet.

Like changing shoes, when she opened the door to the reporter, she became her bright, personable self again. She invited the reporter, who turned out to be a woman, into the living room. Mandy was down for her nap, so it was just the three of them.

Russ stood and shook hands. The woman appeared to be in her mid-thirties, and Russ suspected she thought she was some kind of siren for the local fellows.

"Well, hello there, tall-dark-and-handsome."

"How do you do, Ms. Richards."

"Oh, call me Julia. I can't wait to hear your story. This assignment has been so interesting."

"Has it? You've talked to some of the other bachelors?" he asked, moving back so the woman could be seated.

She sank onto the sofa and patted the space beside

her. "Yes, I have. I've interviewed every couple so far. Come join me so I can hear your story."

Russ sat down. He intended to do whatever Melissa wanted. "Sure. Though you'll need Melissa to help tell the story. This is really about her card company."

"Oh, the focus is supposed to be on the bachelor. You know, a lot of our citizens remember you boys from the ranch."

He turned the conversation back to Melissa's company, insisting she write down its name, and told her about the pictures Melissa had taken.

"I brought my camera to snap a picture of you," Julia assured him.

"You used pictures of the other bachelors?" he asked.

"Oh, yes. All the ladies love to look at a good-looking man," the reporter assured him.

With a sigh, he said, "I think you'd be better off using Melissa's. Show her, sweetheart."

The reporter's eyes narrowed at his words. "My, you two must've really hit it off. You didn't know her before this weekend, did you?"

"No. Sorry, I called her that because of Mandy. It's what I've been calling Mandy all weekend." He hoped that explanation would help.

"Who's Mandy?"

"Melissa's daughter. She's sleeping right now, but she is a real sweetheart."

"I see." The woman turned toward Melissa. "May I see some of the pictures you made of Russ?"

"Yes, of course," Melissa agreed, having sat quietly while he and the reporter talked.

Well, here it came. Once this woman got a gander at the bathtub picture, she'd assume all kinds of things. And then when it appeared in the paper, he'd never hear the end of it.

But he'd accept even that for Melissa.

She came back into the room. "Here are several poses that I think are good."

The reporter took them from Melissa and stared. He steeled himself to be embarrassed.

"You make a good model, Russ, but I prefer a little more, shall we say, beefcake," she said. "Though I wouldn't mind having one of these on my wall."

That wasn't the reaction he'd expected. Frowning, he leaned over to see what pictures she held.

One was of him on Jack. The other was in the barn. There were no bubbles in sight.

CHAPTER TWELVE

IT WAS ALMOST FOUR before the reporter left. She'd insisted on hearing every detail. Then she'd taken several pictures of Russ and Melissa together.

As she was leaving, Russ had given her his business card and asked for a copy of one of the photos. Her gaze had traveled from him to Melissa speculatively, but she'd agreed to send him one.

As soon as the door closed, he turned to Melissa. "Why didn't you give her the bubble pictures?"

Melissa stiffened. "I thought the other two would be better. You know, more a cowboy image."

"That's bull. It was obvious she would've preferred the bathtub shots."

"Okay," Melissa said. "I know that. But you've done everything I asked and more, and I know you weren't happy about having one of those pictures in the paper, so I thought it was the least I could do."

She turned away, but he caught her arm, stopping her. "Thank you, Melissa. I appreciate that."

"No problem. We'll need to leave for the airport in less than an hour. You'd better go pack."

He knew she was eager for him to leave, so she could get her life back in her own control. That much was obvious. But packing would take only a few minutes. "There's plenty of time."

"I need to check on Mandy. It's not normal for her to sleep so long," Melissa said, pulling away.

"You think she might be sick?" Russ asked, concern filling him. He didn't like to think of Mandy being ill.

He was on Melissa's heels when she opened the door to Mandy's bedroom. The baby was still sleeping. Melissa ran her hand gently over her daughter's face.

"Does she have a fever?" Russ whispered.

"She's a little warm. It's probably because she's teething. I'll fix her a water bottle with some baby Tylenol in it." She tiptoed out of the room, leaving Russ standing beside the bed.

Such a little thing. So helpless. That responsibility must weigh heavily on a mother, especially a mother with no support. Again his thoughts turned to his own mother. A sudden flash of being held, comforted, when he didn't feel well came into his head. He shrugged. He must be thinking of Mrs. Duncan.

Or was he? Could he be remembering his own mother? He'd faced the fact that the teddy bear he remembered had come with him to the ranch. He'd once asked Mrs. Duncan who had given it to him. She'd told him he'd been clutching it when he arrived.

For days, he'd tried to ignore that little brown bear. But in the end, he'd taken it back into his bed. He hoped Mandy's bear would bring her as much comfort as his had to him. No matter who had given it to him.

Melissa came back into the room with a bottle in her hand. He stared at it because the liquid was pink.

"Pink water?"

"That's the Tylenol. It's a red liquid."

He took the bottle from her so she could rouse Mandy and lift her from the bed.

"Mandy, it's Mommy. Come on, baby, time to wake up."

Mandy whimpered and rubbed her eyes with her fists. Russ wanted to grab her and cuddle her against him, promise her he'd keep anything from hurting her. Instead, he stood aside and let Melissa take care of her child.

"I'll give her the bottle while you pack," she said softly, after changing Mandy's diaper.

He surrendered the bottle and stood back as the pair left the room. With a shrug, he went to his bedroom to do as Melissa suggested.

After he'd gathered his things together, he joined her in the living room. "Can I have one of the pictures of Mandy and me on Jack?"

"Of course. The packages are on my desk. Feel free to go through and pick one out. I can have another copy made later if I want to use it."

He took the photos into the kitchen and, after wiping off the table, spread them out. There were ten of him and the baby. He loved all of them. Finally, he selected the one that was best of Mandy. He didn't care what he looked like.

He went back into the living room and showed it to Melissa. Mandy shoved the bottle out of her mouth and sat up, reaching for him.

"Da-da-da-da," she cooed.

"Hello, sweetheart. Are you feeling better?" he asked, reaching for her. Melissa released her into his arms.

The baby gurgled and patted his face.

"When will she start to talk?"

Melissa shrugged. "She already says ma-ma and ba-ba. That means bottle," she interpreted for him. "Or ball," she added with a grin. "We practice sometimes, so it shouldn't be too long."

He'd miss that period of her development, he realized. Hell, he was going to miss the rest of her life. Why should it bother him that he wouldn't be here for her first real words? Or her first step. Or her first date.

Frowning, he caressed her pudgy cheeks. "She's such a pretty baby."

Again Melissa smiled. There hadn't been many smiles today. "I certainly won't argue with you there."

"Does she look like her daddy?"

His abrupt question took him by surprise, as well as Melissa.

"I—no, I don't think so. But he was definitely a morning person, like Mandy."

"And me."

"Yes, and you. I should've asked you that before

I planned our weekend, but I didn't. It's fortunate you turned out to be one.''

''Yeah,'' he muttered, his gaze never leaving the baby's face. ''Will she remember me?''

Melissa looked away and shrugged. ''You don't remember your mother at the age of four, Russ. I doubt that Mandy will remember you.''

But he did.

Since coming back to Wyoming and spending time with Melissa and Mandy, he was remembering bits of his early life. Even now, as his heart grew heavy at the thought of leaving Melissa and Mandy, he remembered being clutched tightly in someone's arms, someone who was crying.

His mother.

''She didn't want to leave me,'' he said.

''Who?''

''My mother.''

Melissa hesitated a moment. ''I never thought she did,'' she said quietly.

''I wish I'd realized sooner how...I thought she didn't love me.'' He blinked several times, amazed that tears had filled his eyes.

A warm hand stole into his and he looked at Melissa's pale, soft skin. Her touch filled him with warmth.

''You said she was very young. Sometimes it's easy to think your best isn't good enough, not to realize love is more important than nice clothes or even a full tummy.'' Melissa drew a deep breath and squeezed his hand. ''Maybe you should see if you can track her down. She's probably suffered greatly."

It had never occurred to him that his mother might have suffered. He'd been so angry, so lost, he'd only thought about himself. Then he'd shut thoughts of her away completely.

He kissed Mandy's forehead. "Mandy will always know she's loved."

"Yes. Always."

They sat there in silence, the late-afternoon sun filtering into the room. The peace of the moment filled Russ's heart. He felt better, in many ways, than he ever had. The hurt, the anger that had always been there was easing away. And Melissa's advice to seek out his mother kept repeating itself over and over. Should he?

"It's time to leave for the airport," Melissa said, standing. She held out her arms for her baby. "I'll go change her diaper again, and then we'll go."

Russ reluctantly released the child.

While Melissa changed Mandy, he took his bags to the car. He remembered his arrival, his reluctance to fulfill his promise. He'd been wrong. In the three days he'd spent here, he'd learned a lot. About himself. About life.

On a sudden impulse, he hurried back inside and went to the kitchen, using the wall phone to call the ranch.

"Sam? Has Lindsay returned yet?"

"Not yet, Russ. She'll be back later."

"Do you know anything about my mother?"

Silence followed his question. Finally, Sam cleared his throat. "Nope. But Lindsay has the records."

"Would you ask her to see what she can find and call me in Chicago?"

"'Course I will."

As Russ hung up the phone, feeling a lightheartedness that was completely new to him, Melissa came into the kitchen.

"Did you get everything?" she asked.

"Yeah." Everything he could pack. The picture of him and Mandy was in his garment bag, safely tucked away in his suit pocket. He'd never had pictures in his office, like the other executives. Now he'd proudly display that one. He'd buy a couple of frames, saving one for the picture of him and Melissa that the reporter had promised to send.

They walked together out to the car. He opened the back door and took Mandy from her mother to strap her in her car seat. "Want to go for a ride, little girl?" he asked softly.

Mandy gurgled and jumped back and forth in her seat as he tried to fasten the straps.

"That's one word you understand, isn't it? Go. We're going to go."

She continued to grin up at him, and he tried to memorize her sweetness, to hold it close to his heart to take with him back to Chicago.

Then he stared at Melissa.

He wanted to take her image back to Chicago, too. Her sweetness. Her strength.

The drive to the airport was a silent one.

He couldn't think of anything to say. Should he tell Melissa that he was thinking of taking her advice, of trying to find his mother? No, he hadn't actually made that decision yet. Could he tell her how much he would miss her and Mandy? No. She might get the wrong idea.

After all, he knew she and Mandy didn't fit into his life. His attraction to Melissa had been physical, that was all. He'd find a woman after his return to Chicago. There was that redhead in his office building. They'd chatted a few times.

So he said nothing.

MELISSA CONCENTRATED on her driving. On the traffic. On the advertising billboards along the road. Anything but Russ. If she thought about his leaving, she would cry.

Already she'd cried more than she had since Greg's death. Russ had forced her from her safe cocoon, making her feel again. Making her hurt. Making her become stronger.

In only three days, he'd helped her to be a better person. And a lonelier one. She was going to miss him. Mandy would, too, for a few days.

They got to the airport and she parked the car.

"Don't get out."

She turned to stare at Russ. "What?"

"Don't get out of the car. It's too much trouble with Mandy. I can find my gate okay. It's not like this is O'Hare," he assured her, referring to Chicago's busy airport.

She stared at him. She'd thought she would have a little more time, a few precious minutes waiting for his flight to be called.

But he was right. It was better this way. Abrupt. Clean. Impersonal. "If you insist," she said, pleased that her voice didn't wobble. "Thank you for—for all you've done."

He stared at her, but she couldn't read his expression. She looked out the windshield, hoping he'd hurry and leave while she could still keep their farewell impersonal.

Releasing his seat belt, he slid toward her, not toward the door. She turned to stare at him. "Wha—"

His arms came around her and his lips covered hers. The kiss wasn't like the other two he'd given her, casual, almost incidental. No, this was a full assault on her senses. His lips took over her body and her mind.

Almost without realizing it, she lifted her arms to encircle his neck, cooperating with every breath she had. He pulled away, then repositioned his mouth over hers, deepening the kiss, stroking her tongue with his, her body with his hands.

She clung to his broad shoulders, to his strength, because she felt weak...but never in danger. Russ had her trust. He'd earned it over and over again in his care for Mandy.

In his Mother's Day gift.

In his care for her.

Besides, he was leaving.

So she indulged her craving for his touch, his kiss, without protest. In fact, she responded with all the enthusiasm she could muster. When he pulled back a second time, she protested, her lips enticing him back.

With a groan, he didn't resist. Instead he merely tightened his hold on her body, eliminating any space between them. She couldn't tell where she ended and he began, whether it was her heart thumping loudly or his. She only knew she was in heaven.

It was Mandy's gurgle that parted them.

"Da-da-da-da!" she shrieked as they broke apart.

Russ didn't move far. One thumb caressed her lips as he stared at her. "Melissa…" he whispered.

"You—you'd better go," she whispered in return, forcing herself to pull away from him. "Have a safe trip."

For a minute she thought he wasn't going to move. Then, after dropping another kiss on her lips, a brief one, he opened his car door and got out.

"Can you release the trunk?" he asked, bending down to stare at her.

Such a mundane question after their embrace struck her as funny, but she didn't laugh. "Yes."

She stared in the rearview mirror, catching only glimpses of him as he removed his luggage from the trunk. She realized she wasn't breathing when he walked up to the driver's side of the car.

Taking a deep breath, she rolled down the glass.

He bent over. "Take care of yourself and Mandy."

"I will. You, too."

"Yeah." Again he kissed her. A hard kiss that skipped any preliminary steps. Then he wrenched his mouth from hers and strode away.

She didn't know how long she stared after him. He never turned around. Never looked back. He was gone.

Mandy whimpered, as if she, too, was mourning Russ's departure.

"It's okay, baby," Melissa whispered, looking at her child in the rearview mirror. "We're okay. We're going to be fine."

And she continued to repeat those words over and over again as she drove home.

THE FLIGHT HOME was uneventful.

His apartment looked the same. Boring. Bare. Cold.

He dumped his luggage in his bedroom. Then he picked up the phone and ordered in a pizza. It was there by the time he'd unpacked.

A point in Chicago's favor. You could get food any time of the day or night. And fast. If he'd gone out early this morning in Chicago to find a present for Melissa, he wouldn't have been limited to nail polish, either.

Chicago had everything.

Except Melissa and Mandy.

He intended to put that thought from his mind. But

the picture of him and Mandy was on his breakfast table. Tomorrow he'd buy a frame, so his precious picture would be protected.

Then he gathered his mail, checked his answering machine and prepared for life in the big city.

AFTER LUNCH THE NEXT DAY, he unwrapped the silver frame he'd bought. In seconds, he'd slid the picture of him and Mandy into the frame and had it sitting on his credenza.

He only had to turn his head to see the baby again. To feel the warmth of her little body against him. To remember her mother and those goodbye kisses at the airport. To wonder how he was going to live without them.

"Hey, Russ, glad you're back. How did—" The tall man who'd stuck his head into Russ's office straightened abruptly. "Whoa! Who's that?" he asked, moving into the office, his gaze on the picture.

"You don't recognize me?"

"Not with a baby in your arms. You changing your mind about children?"

Mike Wilson was a friend. Or at least an acquaintance. They were both without family and went out together occasionally.

Russ shrugged his shoulders. "I spent the weekend with her, and she's a sweetheart."

"Yeah, lots of them are for an hour or two. You'd change your mind quickly enough if you hung around a baby very long."

"Is that why you don't see your child?" Russ

asked quietly. He knew Mike was divorced. He'd moved from Dallas and seldom mentioned the woman and child he'd left behind.

"Hey, buddy, don't get any weird ideas. I pay for my freedom. That woman would haul me into court if I missed even one payment."

Russ had never questioned Mike's attitude before. Now he felt sick to his stomach. He didn't even know the woman, but his sympathies lay with her.

He tried to hide his reaction.

"Say, the reason I stopped in was to see if you're free tonight," Mike continued. "You know that little redhead you've been eyeing? I ran into her and a girlfriend on Saturday. She expressed an interest in you."

Russ remembered his plans. He'd intended to make a connection with her after his weekend in Wyoming. Why did it hold so little appeal now?

"And, man," Mike continued, "she's hot to trot for you. Her girlfriend isn't bad, either. Patty. She's blond and has big—" He paused and held out his hands, palms up. "So how about tonight?"

Russ cleared his throat. "I'm a little behind since I was off Friday. Why don't we make it another night."

"When? Tomorrow? I want to strike while the iron is hot. My bed has been empty for a few nights. Time for a little action."

Had *he* been this shallow? Russ wondered. This disgusting? No. Perhaps he hadn't been as caring and sensitive as he should've been, but he hadn't used women the way Mike was talking about doing.

"I can't this week, Mike. Sorry."

"So shall I schedule it for Saturday night? That'd give you plenty of time to catch up."

"No, thanks."

Mike stared at him, his hands on his hips. "What's wrong with you, man? Did you suddenly become a stick-in-the-mud?"

Russ couldn't answer him. He couldn't explain the changes he was experiencing. But he knew why. Melissa and Mandy.

Mandy's father was dead. He'd had no choice about leaving his child. If he'd walked away from Mandy, as Mike had with his child, Russ would now be trying to look him up and plant a facer on him.

With Mike staring at him, he finally said, "I'm not interested, Mike."

The man stiffened. "I think I get the picture. See you around, Hall." He stalked out of the office.

Russ leaned back in his chair, trying to figure out what had just happened. Had he changed that much? He hadn't done a lot with Mike in the last year. Things had always come up. Had he been distancing himself from the man without realizing it?

Or had Mandy and Melissa had such an effect on his life that he'd changed almost overnight? His gaze went to the picture of him and Mandy.

He wondered if she was feeling better. Had her fever come back? Had Melissa been able to get up this morning a little more easily since she'd gotten to sleep in the past three mornings?

Had she chosen the pictures for the cards?

Did they miss him?

He reached for the phone.

CHAPTER THIRTEEN

MELISSA GROANED and flopped back against the pillow. It wasn't the getting up early that disturbed her.

It was her dreams.

She'd tossed and turned all night, dreaming of Russ, of his touch. The man was driving her crazy. Mandy had been cranky last night, after their return from the airport. Easy to blame it on her teething.

But Melissa believed her baby missed Russ. Just as she did. Damn the man. He came into their lives, got them all stirred up, and then waltzed out again.

"And it's all my fault," she muttered to herself. After all, she'd invited him to stay in her house. But she hadn't known how caring he could be. Or how much fun. He'd teased her a lot. Made her laugh.

And it certainly wasn't a hardship to look at his body, either.

A shudder raced through her as she remembered those kisses at the airport. It was a good thing he'd walked away, or she might've pleaded with him not to go.

Which was silly. He didn't want marriage and a ready-made family.

Mandy called to her, and Melissa knew her option

of remaining in bed had just been canceled. "Coming, sweetie," she called, shrugging on her robe.

Her day had begun.

AFTER PICKING UP MANDY from Mrs. Tuttle, Melissa came back home that evening, exhausted. Why? She hadn't done any more than she usually did.

But she'd gone through her day missing Russ.

It was ridiculous. The man had only been here three days. She and Mandy had managed without anyone for a much longer time.

She carried Mandy to the kitchen and put her in the high chair. Feeding her was first on the list. As she took down several jars of baby food, she caught the blinking light on the answering machine.

She kept it on the kitchen counter instead of in her office because otherwise she often forgot to check it. Probably something at the office. She'd left a little early to pick up the other pictures she'd taken of Russ. The ones in his tux.

Though she'd glanced at them briefly, she intended to wait until after Mandy had been fed to take a good look at them. That way she could enjoy them.

She hit the play button on her way to the table. A recorded sales message started playing. With a sigh, she opened the baby food and began feeding Mandy.

But she froze after the beep when the next message started.

"Melissa? You there?" Russ asked.

He paused and Mandy started babbling, looking around the room.

"He's not here, baby," Melissa hurriedly said, as if her daughter could understand.

"I guess you're not there," his deep voice continued. "I was wondering how Mandy felt. And you, too. I wanted to tell you I bought a frame for the picture you gave me. And that I had a great weekend. I'll try to call later this evening to see how Mandy's doing. Bye."

Melissa slowly let out her pent-up breath. She picked up the spoon again to feed Mandy and discovered her hands were shaking. If the man could disturb her that much with his voice, think what would happen if he suddenly appeared.

She'd best be grateful that there was no possibility of him coming back. There was no future for him here. Their life-styles didn't mesh. And she wasn't ready to take another man into her life.

A vision of Russ settled in her heart and she stared into space. No. No, she wasn't. It would hurt too much. But what did that matter, she realized. It already hurt too much, anyway.

Mandy pounded on the tray of her high chair, demanding her mother's attention.

"Yes, sweetie, I'm here. Open up." She wished she could be like her daughter, easily assuaged with food. But she had no appetite. Only heartache.

After bathing Mandy, Melissa put her to bed at the normal time. Then she began doing the household chores that filled her evenings, followed by work she'd brought home from the office.

She dreaded going to bed, sure she would dream

of Russ again. Determined to ward off that misery, she crawled into bed with a mystery she thought she might like. But after reading the first page four times, she realized the book wasn't enough to distract her.

She'd shut off the lamp by her bed and lay staring at the ceiling when the phone rang.

"Melissa? Is it too late to call? I worked late and lost track of the time," Russ said as soon as she answered.

A frightening sense of homecoming filled her. Russ had called. "No, it's not too late. I was just reading. How was your flight home?"

"Boring. How's Mandy?"

"Fine. Her fever didn't come back."

"Good."

An awkward silence filled the air.

"Did you have a lot of work waiting for you?" she finally asked.

"Yeah. We're starting a new office building. I spent a lot of time in meetings this afternoon."

"That sounds interesting."

"It was. Tell me what you did with your day."

Though she thought her day had been mundane, she gave him the details. She told him about the pictures she'd picked up, assuring him he looked great.

"Did the article come out in the paper today?"

"No, I believe it will be out on Wednesday. I'll send you a copy of it."

"Do you have my address?"

"I have your office address. I can send it there."

"Okay. Let me give you some numbers where I

can be reached. If you and Mandy need anything—call me."

She couldn't do that. Russ lived in Chicago. He wasn't a part of their lives. But she didn't tell him that. After dutifully writing down the numbers, she thanked him again for all he'd done.

"I think I owe you," he said softly. "I'll let you get to sleep now. Take care."

"You, too."

After hanging up the phone, she closed her eyes. She knew she'd dream of him now after hearing his sexy voice while she lay in bed. She couldn't help it.

But she knew in her heart he wouldn't call her again.

RUSS CALLED HER every night.

He spent the entire day trying to think of a good excuse. Tuesday it was because he thought he'd left a belt there. He found it later in his closet, but he didn't look until after his phone call.

Wednesday he called to find out about the article in the newspaper. Thursday he wanted to ask if she'd chosen the pictures she intended to use.

Friday he wanted to tell her about a movie he'd seen the night before. A movie to keep him from going insane until he could call her.

Saturday, he called to discuss his decision to search for his mother. He'd talked to Lindsay and she'd promised to help him get the files of his placement at the ranch.

"Russ, that's wonderful," Melissa said. "I think you've made the right decision."

The warmth of her voice seemed to travel the phone wires like a physical thing, enveloping him as he sat on his couch. "I wish we had those television phones," he said.

"Why? You know what I look like."

"Yeah. But what are you wearing?"

Embarrassed silence was his only answer.

"Melissa? What are you wearing?"

"Um, I was changing when the phone rang. If it had been a video phone, I wouldn't have answered."

He tried to smother his groan as a wave of desire shot through him at the thought of Melissa half-dressed. "Are you and Mandy going out?" he asked, to change the subject.

"We're going to the office for a little while. I have a bit more work to do on the cards before I can send them to the printer. I'm anxious to get them finished."

"You'll send me some?"

"Of course. You'll get the first copy of every card."

"I think I might be coming back to Wyoming for a few days real soon." The plan had just popped into his head.

"Really?" She drew a deep breath that had him practically panting. "Why?"

"Business. You don't sound happy about it."

"I—it has nothing to do with me, Russ. I mean, I know you'd be busy."

"Not too busy to see you and Mandy."

"We'd love to see you, too," she said in a rush.

"Great. I'll let you know when."

He hung up the phone after telling her goodbye and began pacing his apartment. He hadn't lied to her. He had business in Wyoming. But it would have nothing to do with the company he worked for.

Since he'd come back to Chicago, he'd felt like a caged tiger. He'd paced his office. He'd paced his apartment. He'd paced the sidewalks.

His time here was over. He'd finally realized that last night. He longed to be back in Casper. And the longing only got worse as each day passed.

He'd found the sketches of the house he'd done that night in Melissa's kitchen. He'd begun drawing up actual plans. This was his house, and he intended to build it. In Casper.

His plans were half-formed, but he knew he was headed in the right direction.

The house would be perfect, but only if it held Melissa and Mandy, he finally admitted. He'd known that all along, but he hadn't been willing to acknowledge the source of the need that clawed at him.

He'd never been able to commit to a woman before. Never been able to bear the risk of her leaving him. He'd thought if he didn't love anyone, he wouldn't be hurt.

But Melissa—and Mandy—had sneaked up on him. He knew he had strong feelings for them. He just didn't know if it was love. But whatever it was, he wanted to be with them, to share in their lives.

Not that he intended to say anything yet. He'd move back to Wyoming, build his home, spend more time with the Bright ladies. Then he'd let Melissa know that she was important to him.

He chose the next weekend for his trip to Casper. Each night, when he talked to Melissa, he made plans. They were going to go out to the ranch and ride. Mandy needed an opportunity to wear those little blue jeans he'd bought her.

A picnic was on the schedule, with Melissa promising to provide the food. He'd even dared ask her to arrange baby-sitting with Mrs. Tuttle so they could have another evening out, just the adults.

"I don't know. Mrs. Tuttle said her niece is coming to visit," Melissa had replied, hesitating.

"Maybe another neighbor could keep an eye on Mandy." He wanted to dance with Melissa again, to feel her against him.

"I'll see."

Thursday morning as he worked at his desk, the phone rang. He picked it up, in a cheery mood since he'd be seeing Melissa Friday night. "Russ Hall," he said.

After a moment of silence, a female voice asked, "Is this Russ Hall from Wyoming?"

He knew at once who was calling. He'd discovered a register for adopted children and their birth parents. Information was exchanged if both parties were listed.

He hadn't expected to hear anything so soon.

"Yes." His heart was racing. Something in the voice struck a memory, a long-forgotten memory.

"I—I'm—this is your m-mother." The voice shook with suppressed emotion.

The only word he could manage was "Yes."

"You—you r-registered—" The woman broke into sobs.

Russ wanted to speak, to offer solace, but he didn't know what to say. Before he could manage to reply, he heard a scuffling noise, then a strong male voice came in the line.

"Hello."

"Hello? Who's this?" Russ demanded.

"I'm Emily's husband. Is this Russ?"

"Yes."

"Look, I know this isn't easy for you, but Emily's been tearing herself up over contacting you. Do you really want to know your mother?"

Here was the turning point. Even when he'd registered, he hadn't been sure. He wanted to know whether or not his mother was out there. But was he really ready to meet her?

"Yes," he uttered again, his voice cracking with emotion.

"Are you willing to come to our house?"

"Where do you live?" Russ asked, frowning. He'd travel anywhere, but he'd planned to go to Wyoming this weekend.

"Here, in Chicago."

Russ gasped, unable to believe that he and his

mother had lived in the same city all these years. "Give me the address."

After writing it down, he said, "I'll be there in half an hour, if that's all right."

The man assured him they'd be waiting.

HE HADN'T CALLED.

Melissa had known she was depending too much on Russ's nightly calls. She waited each evening, curled up in her bed, her gaze on the phone.

It was madness. She needed to put him out of her thoughts. There was no future for her with Russ.

But still she waited.

It was past 2:00 a.m. He obviously wasn't calling tonight. She was an idiot to still be awake, still aching to hear his voice. Longing to know that he thought of her as he went through his day, as she thought of him.

She'd bought two picture frames. She'd put one of the photos of Russ in his tux in the first frame. It sat beside her bed so she could look at it while she talked to him.

The other frame held a picture of him and Mandy. It was in her daughter's room, and each day she showed it to Mandy.

What was she doing? she wondered now. Setting up her daughter's heart to be broken as well as her own? What kind of a mother was she?

One who wanted her daughter to know and love Russ Hall as much as she did.

That was ridiculous. They'd known each other for

such a short time. But that time had been spent exchanging thoughts, sharing laughter, caring for each other. She knew Russ cared for her and Mandy. His phone calls told her that.

But did he love them? Both of them?

She didn't know.

She looked again at the phone, then at the clock. With a weary sigh, she turned off the lamp and fell back against the pillow.

Maybe tomorrow.

THE PHONE RANG BEFORE she left for work the next day.

"Melissa, it's Russ."

"Russ! How are you? I was afraid—"

"I have bad news."

She hadn't expected those words. In fact, she'd already noted a buoyant note in his voice, as if something exciting had happened. "What—"

"I can't come to Wyoming this weekend."

Her heart fell. She hadn't realized how much she'd been looking forward to seeing him again. She struggled to remain calm, not to let him hear her disappointment. "I'm sorry. Is anything wrong?"

"We've run into some snags on the project and I'm going to have to put in five or six hours on Saturday."

"I see. Well, maybe some other time."

"Damn it, Melissa, I don't want to wait," he protested, sounding frustrated.

"I don't, either." His honesty deserved the same in return.

"Good. I've changed the reservation to your name. I'll meet you at the airport."

Stunned, she stared into space, unprepared for his request. Or order. "I—I can't. Mandy—"

"Ask Mrs. Tuttle to take her for the weekend. Or, I know, I'll call Lindsay. She'll take care of her."

"No! I can't just dump my child because—" Because she was crazy about a man? Because she wanted to start living again? She had a responsibility to Mandy. She loved Mandy.

"Melissa, we won't have a lot of time. But I need to see you. I want to see Mandy, too, but the trip would be too hard on both of you. Please come this time by yourself?"

She heard another voice in the background. "What was that?"

"I'm holding up a meeting. I have to go. Please come."

"I'll let you know," she said quietly, then hung up the phone.

"Ma-ma-ma-ma!" Mandy called, waving at her from the high chair.

"Yes, baby, Mommy's here," she said, kissing her daughter on the forehead. Yes. She'd always be here. For Mandy.

She sat still, beside her child, her mind going round and round as she debated her choices. A knock at the door surprised her.

When she opened the door, she found Mrs. Tuttle

standing there, accompanied by a woman in her fifties. Melissa stepped back and invited them in. "You must be the niece Mrs. Tuttle has been expecting."

"Yes, I'm Natalie. I've heard so much about you and your baby, I couldn't wait to meet you." The woman smiled warmly and shook Melissa's hand.

"Where is baby Mandy? I explained to Natalie that we're keeping her tomorrow night when Russ comes back. It will be so much fun."

Melissa looked at Mrs. Tuttle, sure her face revealed her distress. But she couldn't help it. "He's not coming."

"What? That dear boy isn't coming? Why? Something must be wrong or I know he would be here."

Melissa nodded, finding it difficult to speak. A sense of mourning filled her. It was ridiculous to be so upset over canceled plans. But she was.

"He—he has to work. He wanted me to come to Chicago, but I can't leave Mandy. I just can't." She turned and headed for the kitchen, gesturing for her guests to follow. "Come meet Mandy."

While the two ladies were cooing and smiling at her child, Melissa put on water for coffee. When she carried cups to the table, the two ladies sat down with her.

"Now, what's this about you not going to see Russ?" Mrs. Tuttle demanded, her voice firm.

Melissa tried to smile. She didn't feel her attempt was completely successful. "Russ invited me, but I said no, of course."

"What do you mean, of course? Of course you'll go."

"Mrs. Tuttle—"

"Natalie and I would love to take care of Mandy. With Natalie here, you don't have to worry about me getting too tired. She watches over me like a mother hen. In fact, having someone else for her to look after would suit her to a tee."

"She's right, you know," Natalie chimed in. "My two are grown. I'm a widow like Aunt Cathy, so I'd love the chance to spoil a baby again."

"When are you supposed to go?" Mrs. Tuttle asked.

"I don't know. He said he made reservations in my name but he didn't give me a time." When the elderly lady reached for the phone, Melissa tried to pull herself together. "Mrs. Tuttle, I can't—"

Mrs. Tuttle ignored her. After looking up the number in the directory, she called the Casper airport. "What flights do you have for Chicago this evening?" There was a moment's pause, then she said briskly, "Please check the six-forty-five and see if you have a reservation for Melissa Bright. My husband said he'd made me a reservation, but he forgot to tell me the flight number."

Melissa stared wide-eyed. She'd never seen Mrs. Tuttle take charge like this.

Natalie spoke softly. "Aunt Cathy believes you and Russ are perfect for each other. She could scarcely talk of anything else."

"But—we're not—"

Mrs. Tuttle hung up the phone. "You're on the six-forty-five flight. We'll leave for the airport at five, so be packed and ready."

Melissa stared at the other two women, her blood already racing at the thought of seeing Russ again.

"I shouldn't leave my baby," she began, but Mrs. Tuttle would have none of that.

"Pooh! Every couple needs time alone. We're going to take good care of your baby."

"But we're not really a couple, Mrs. Tuttle," Melissa protested, even as her heart urged her to go.

"Not yet, but you will be. How else are you going to make those babies?"

CHAPTER FOURTEEN

MRS. TUTTLE AND NATALIE took her to the airport that afternoon. She'd told them not to get out, as Russ had done, and had gone to the airport counter alone.

"I have a reservation on the six-forty-five flight to Chicago," she told the ground attendant, laying a credit card down to pay for the ticket.

"Your name?"

After giving her name, she waited, tense, as the woman checked her flight list. "Oh, yes, Ms. Bright. You're in first class, seat four."

"First class? There must be a mistake. I want tourist class."

"Well, if you insist, but we'll have to give you a refund, and it will all be rather complicated."

"But I haven't paid for it yet."

"Your ticket was paid in Chicago. By a Mr. Hall."

Melissa chewed on her bottom lip. Finally, she nodded. "Okay."

"So you want to move to tourist class?"

"No. I'll take first class."

The lady smiled at her. "Good." She printed up the ticket and handed it to her. "Have a nice flight."

Melissa entered the gate area, wondering if she'd made a mistake. She wanted to see Russ so badly. Mandy would be safe. She could enjoy her weekend. But was she setting herself up for more heartache?

All the way to Chicago, she questioned her decision. Several times she thought she should get back on a return flight as soon as this one landed.

The argument raged on and on, giving her a headache. It was the strength of her desire to see him that bothered her the most. It was stronger than a dying man's thirst for water. Two weeks without him and she was falling apart.

The debate ended as soon as she emerged from the tunnel and saw him standing head and shoulders above the crowd. Then need took over and she flew into his waiting arms.

He kissed her with an intensity that left both of them breathless. Then he kissed her with a gentleness that filled her heart.

With one arm wrapped around her, he took her carry-on bag in his other and started toward the baggage claim.

"I don't have any other luggage," she said.

"All the better," he muttered, pulling her tighter against his big frame.

Melissa scarcely had eyes for the crowds at the airport, the bustling streets and soaring skyscrapers. All she could do was stare at Russ.

He held her hand the entire drive. When they

stopped at red lights, he kissed her long after the lights changed, until cars honked in protest. But they didn't speak.

After leaving his car in a nearby parking garage, he led her to the lobby of his apartment building. Alone in the elevator, he pulled her into his embrace and kissed her until the door slid open ten floors up.

Then, with the turn of a key, they were in his apartment, alone, separated from the world.

"Are you hungry? Do you need food?" Russ asked. "I made you a reservation at the hotel across the street."

She was astounded. It hadn't occurred to her that she wouldn't be staying with him, probably because he'd stayed with her. Of course, a hotel room. That was the sensible thing.

She shook her head no.

"No food?" he repeated, his gaze never leaving hers.

She shook her head again.

Without a word, they moved toward each other at the same time. Once again in his arms, Melissa found it impossible to think about anything else but Russ.

He finally pulled back, staring at her. "Melissa, we have to stop now—or I won't be able to. I want you too badly," he whispered.

Melissa's initial response was to beg him not to stop. She wanted him. The intensity of her desire stunned her.

She'd thought she would always be true to Greg. But with a flash of comprehension, she realized she was a different woman now. Older, more mature, more experienced. Her capacity for love was greater now. She would always cherish Greg's memory. After all, he'd given her Mandy.

But she could still love. And the recipient of that love, Russ, was standing right before her.

"I want you, too," she murmured, drawing his mouth down to hers.

He didn't wait for a second request. Sweeping her into his arms, he hurried through his apartment to his bedroom.

Melissa didn't notice the decor. Her world began and ended in Russ's embrace. He placed her on the bed and lay down beside her, kissing and stroking her until she couldn't think. She could only respond.

They undressed each other quickly, eager to have no barriers between them.

"Melissa, I've dreamed of holding you like this," Russ whispered, running his hands over her soft skin, leaving a trail of heat.

"I did, too," she murmured, unable to describe the agony of longing she'd felt since he'd left Casper. Each night she'd grown more and more feverish as she'd imagined them together, naked, reveling in each other's touch. The reality transcended her most erotic dreams.

His large hands cradled her breasts, drawing a heated response. She moaned and pressed closer as his mouth replaced his hands. As she felt his arousal against her leg, an ache welled up deep within her, a need that could only be fulfilled by Russ.

"Now, Russ. Now," she pleaded.

"In a minute, Melissa," he whispered, before his mouth took hers again.

The sweet ache only grew, drawing Melissa deeper and deeper in the vortex of desire. It was impossible to discover where she ended and Russ began. Whether she gave pleasure or received it. Who led or who followed.

When he pulled away, she panicked, thinking he'd changed his mind. But he'd withdrawn to get protection, putting on a condom before reaching for her again.

When he entered her, Melissa's mind was wiped as blank as a slate. Sensation took over and the need within her reached such an intensity she thought she couldn't bear any more. With a rising surge of pleasure, she climaxed, her response rippling through her body in shuddering waves of release.

Russ collapsed against her, the strong muscles of his back rising and falling beneath her hands. Her hold on him tightened, keeping him close. She needed to feel him against her. Needed to know he had shared in the overwhelming intensity of their lovemaking.

Russ didn't resist. Instead, he wrapped his arms around her, sliding to her side and pulling her with him. His lips traced warm kisses over her face.

A tear slid from Melissa's eyes and tracked down her cheek to land on Russ's shoulder. Not a tear of regret, but a tear of ecstasy. A tear of completion, a tear of oneness.

GUILT SLAMMED INTO RUSS as he felt that tear. He'd rushed her. Their time together had been short. She thought she still loved Mandy's father. Had Russ forced her into intimacy before she was ready?

Had he hurt her?

He tightened his hold, fearful she'd pull away. "Melissa, don't cry. I didn't intend—I didn't mean to pressure you. I lost control. But I'll do better, I promise. Everything will be all right. We won't—because we slept together once doesn't mean—"

She gave no response, other than to continue lying in his arms. He ran a hand through her soft, dark hair, soothing and caressing, hoping to lull her into a feeling of safety, of happiness, banishing any regrets. He held his breath, fearing she would break away. Finally forced to draw in air, he pulled back briefly to note her closed eyes. He stretched one long arm to pull a sheet over their cooling bodies, then resumed their embrace.

He closed his own eyes, living his dream of holding Melissa close to him all through the night.

When he awoke, she was still pressed against him, her body warm and pliant. His immediate physical response was overwhelming, but he carefully edged away from her, denying his need. He couldn't take her again before he talked to her, apologized for rushing her, let her know his feelings.

He now knew his plan of returning to Wyoming and courting Melissa for a number of months, of giving himself time to adjust to the idea of marriage, was a lot of bull.

His need was immediate, and it was not the need of a man for sex. That need could be satisfied by other women. What he felt for Melissa was love. He needed to love her, to share her life, to love her child.

Forever.

And heaven help him if she didn't feel the same way.

He tucked the cover around her, hoping she'd sleep late and enjoy a rare lazy morning. He'd like that morning to include him. But not today. There would be other mornings he'd share with Melissa. He had to believe that.

Leaving a note beside the coffeepot, he departed an hour later for the office to put in the overtime to which he'd committed himself yesterday. The sooner he got his work done, the sooner he'd return to Melissa.

MELISSA SLOWLY CAME AWAKE, a feeling of deep-seated satisfaction filling her. Why was this morning special? she asked herself before she even opened her eyes. Almost before she processed the question, the answer was there as Russ's scent wafted over her.

But she was alone.

She opened her eyes and sat up, clutching the cover to her naked body. They'd made love. This time, it wasn't a dream, but a stunning reality.

Like a patient testing the soreness of a wound, Melissa again thought of Greg and the love they'd shared. It was still there, would always be there because of Mandy.

But the oneness she'd shared with Russ was more. More passionate, more exciting, overwhelming. She was a fortunate woman to have found and loved two men in her life.

A vague recollection of Russ's response after their lovemaking brought a frown to her lips. She'd been almost asleep, wrapped in his arms, reveling in the warm glow of their lovemaking, when he'd spoken. Her eyelids had been too heavy to open.

At the time, she'd let the caressing tones of his voice wash over her, not really paying attention to what he said. But now his words were coming back. *I didn't intend—I didn't mean to—I lost control.*

Uncertain about the meaning of his words, she felt reluctant to stay in the bed where they'd made love. Instinctively, she padded to the kitchen.

And found his note.

Melissa,
Have to go to the office and work. Should be home by noon. We can have lunch, then check you into the hotel. I have lots to tell you.

Russ

She checked her watch, a sense of panic filling her. It was after nine. He was coming at noon to take her to a hotel. As if they hadn't shared any intimacy the night before.

Again his words after they'd made love came back to her. They seemed more sinister this time, since he was moving her out of his apartment. *He hadn't intended for them to make love.*

Obviously when she'd shown herself to be so willing, he'd given in to temptation. And regretted it.

She chewed on her bottom lip as she thought about last night. More than his words, she remembered his tone of voice. It had been loving, comforting, as in her dreams. So why was he offering to take her to a hotel?

Could he possibly think she didn't want him? "I must be more out of practice than I thought," she said to herself with a rueful chuckle. When he got back at noon, they would talk. As they should've done last night. She wasn't moving to a hotel. If he didn't want her, she'd go home. But she hoped her instincts were right and she'd feel those warm arms around her again.

After a shower in his ultramodern bathroom, Melissa got dressed. Then she wandered into the kitchen, wondering if she should prepare lunch. She opened the refrigerator door and laughed. Typical bachelor fare—a couple of eggs, some cheese dip, three Cokes and a bottle of ketchup. Experienced cook that she was, even she couldn't concoct a meal out of those ingredients.

While she was thinking about finding a neighborhood grocery, if such a thing existed in downtown Chicago, the phone rang. Her first thought was of Russ and she hurried to pick it up. Then she saw the answering machine sitting beside it on the breakfast bar. She decided to let the machine take the call in case it wasn't him.

"Russ, darling," a throaty, feminine voice sounded, causing Melissa's heart to contract. "Thursday evening was one of the most wonderful in my life. You made me so happy. I love you. Please call."

Melissa felt as if she'd turned to stone.

Russ was involved with another woman.

He'd made love to her last night...had sex with her last night, she amended...but he'd been with another woman on Thursday. The pain that pierced her heart was unbearable.

That he could betray her in such a way proved how little she knew him. How wrong she'd been about him.

Even worse, the love, the hunger in the other woman's voice matched her own. More than the words in the message, it was the depth of emotion in the voice that told Melissa the woman cared about Russ more than he deserved.

She understood just how she felt.

She didn't know how long she stood there, feeling more and more bereft. Finally, she trudged to the bedroom. First she straightened the bed, hoping that its sterile neatness would erase her memories of the previous night.

After repacking her bag, she, too, wrote a note.

Russ,
Thanks for the offer of a weekend, but I think

I'll go home. I don't belong in a big city like
this. Besides, I miss Mandy. Thanks again.
                                    Melissa

She carefully replaced his note with hers, then
folded the one he'd written and tucked it in her purse.
She called the airline and changed her reservation
before heading for the elevator with her bag.

MELISSA DIDN'T BOTHER to call Mrs. Tuttle to let her
know she'd be home early. For one thing, she didn't
think she could discuss her change of plans without
crying.

She'd been able to hold in the hurt and heartache
because she hadn't had to say anything other than
tell the clerk what flight she'd switched to. Otherwise, she followed directions and nodded when necessary. If anyone asked what was wrong, she was
afraid her misery would come spewing out like Old
Faithful, the famous geyser in Yellowstone.

She closed her eyes on the plane, her face turned
toward the window so no one would attempt to chat
with her. She suspected her ghostly paleness, something she'd noted in the mirror in Russ's elegant
bathroom, had as much to do with holding people at
bay as her silence did.

By the time the plane landed, a leaden sadness had
filled her, settling her jittery nerves but leaving her
with no less an ache inside. But she felt more in
control.

She exited the airport and waved for the first taxi.

Her home wasn't too far from the airport, and she viewed the house with desperate eyes. Could she forget what had happened, what she'd done, now that she was back in her own comfortable world?

Or would she be forever haunted by the love she'd lost?

After paying the taxi driver, she unlocked her house and entered the familiar surroundings. The familiar silent surroundings. Mandy was with Mrs. Tuttle and Natalie, of course.

The silence, however, seemed symbolic of her life. She collapsed on her sofa, the tears she'd held back no longer denied. Burying her face in her arms, she sobbed her heart out for all she'd lost.

Finally, she sat up and wiped her face. She hadn't gotten through those difficult times after Greg's death by crying, she reminded herself. She could survive this blow also.

And she'd think twice before risking her heart again.

She and Mandy would have a good life. Her company was going to do well, thanks in part to Russ. Her life would be full, she assured herself.

After washing her face, she walked next door. It was time to bring Mandy home and get on with her life.

Mrs. Tuttle answered her knock, a surprised expression on her face. "Why, Melissa, what are you doing home so early?"

"Russ had to work and I missed Mandy too much to stay all weekend. How is she?"

"Why, she's fine, dear. Come right in. It's lunchtime and Natalie is feeding her chicken and rice and carrots, her favorites. We've prepared sandwiches for us. I'll fix you one, too."

Before Melissa could protest that she couldn't eat anything, Mrs. Tuttle rushed ahead of her to the kitchen. She followed, desperately needing to see her daughter.

"Ma-ma-ma-ma!" Mandy shrieked when Melissa entered, reaching out her little arms.

Melissa thought all her tears had been shed, but Mandy's reception touched her heart. "Oh, baby, I missed you so," she exclaimed, kissing the top of Mandy's head. "How are you?"

"She's got carrots smeared all over her. Be careful," Natalie warned cheerfully. "What are you doing home? Didn't trust us with Mandy?"

"Of course I did," Melissa replied, not wanting to hurt the women's feelings. "But I missed her, and Russ had more work than he'd thought. So I came home."

She was determined to keep her explanation simple and as close to the truth as she could.

"You could've gone sightseeing," Mrs. Tuttle suggested. "You've never been there before. I went to the Art Institute once. It's a fine museum." She was busily preparing another sandwich.

"Yes, I've heard it is. But I really did miss Mandy."

Natalie smiled. "I can understand that. She's a wonderful child. So happy."

"Yes, I'm very fortunate." Melissa meant that—and intended to keep reminding herself of her good fortune. She wouldn't fall into the trap again of becoming a martyr. She and her child would live life joyfully. Without Russ.

"Here, child, sit down and eat. You look tired," Mrs. Tuttle said with a frown.

"I don't care for air travel," Melissa told her, hoping those words would explain her pale face and red eyes.

Natalie told a tale about getting airsick, but Melissa barely heard it. Her mind raced with thoughts of the past twenty-four hours.

When the phone rang, she looked at her watch. Almost twelve-thirty. Russ would be home by now. But he didn't know Mrs. Tuttle's number. It couldn't be him.

Mrs. Tuttle answered the phone.

"Why, yes, Russ, she's right here."

And she handed the phone to Melissa.

CHAPTER FIFTEEN

RUSS HELD HIS BREATH until he heard Melissa's voice. After he'd arrived home from the office and read her note, he'd been afraid he'd lost her completely.

"Melissa? Are you all right?" he asked now.

"Yes."

Her voice sounded weak, as if she were ill.

"Sweetheart, what happened? Why did you leave? I don't understand."

"I'm having lunch with Mrs. Tuttle and Natalie."

It took him a moment to realize the non sequitur was her way of telling him she couldn't talk in front of other people.

Okay. "How's Mandy?"

"She's fine."

Frustration filled him. He knew he wasn't going to get much conversation out of her while she was at Mrs. Tuttle's. And probably not when she was home, either. Something had gone wrong, and she didn't want to talk to him.

It didn't take much guessing to figure out what that something was. He'd rushed her, taking her to bed the minute she got within touching distance. He should have known she needed more time, but all he had thought of was his burning need for her.

"Melissa—"

"I have to go now."

"Right." What else could he say? Insist she talk to him? There was no time. Before he could say anything else, she hung up the phone.

It didn't matter, anyway. This wasn't something that could be resolved over the phone. He dialed another number and asked for the first plane heading to Casper.

He intended to be on it.

"IS EVERYTHING ALL RIGHT?" Natalie asked. "You look pale."

"Everything's fine. Mandy and I need to go home."

"Now, dearie, you sit down and eat your sandwich," Mrs. Tuttle insisted. "You don't want to pass out. You might be carrying Mandy."

With a sigh, Melissa sat back down. Fine. She'd eat. What difference did it make, anyway? She'd never hear from Russ again.

She'd known it was over when she heard the other woman's voice. No wonder Russ had made sure he'd had a condom at hand.

Well, she was home. And she'd stay home. No more gallivanting off to strange cities, no chasing after dreams, no—

"Did Russ finish his work?"

Melissa stared at Mrs. Tuttle, trying to understand her question. ''Oh. Oh, yes, he did.''

''I bet he wishes you'd stayed,'' Mrs. Tuttle said with a chuckle. ''You know, they have a great aquarium right there on the lake. You could've seen that, too.''

''Yes.'' Melissa took a bite of her sandwich in self-defense. Until she ate something, she'd be stuck here making conversation, when all she wanted to do was hide.

''When will Russ come for another visit?''

''I doubt that he will. He was only here because of the auction, remember? That's all finished, so I imagine he'll get on with his life in Chicago. He has an interesting job, you know.'' She was babbling like an idiot.

''What kind of work does he do?'' Natalie asked.

Melissa barely got through the next half hour, each agonizing moment of it. Finally, she thanked Mrs. Tuttle for her lunch and gathered Mandy and her belongings. ''Thank you so much for keeping her while I was gone. I don't know what I'd do without you.''

Mrs. Tuttle hugged her. ''That's what grannies are for, Melissa. I may only be an honorary granny, but I take my job seriously.''

Melissa tried a smile. ''Mandy couldn't have a better granny.''

''And I'll be just as good a granny to your other children. After all, Russ doesn't have a mother, either.''

Melissa stared at the elderly lady, her heart breaking all over again at the loss of her dreams.

THE FLIGHT TO CASPER seemed incredibly slow. Russ wanted to get out and push the plane to speed things up. He'd realized something had gone wrong, of course, but Melissa's voice had him even more worried.

He wanted to reassure her, to beg her to forgive him, to hold her.

He gave himself a stern warning. That was the reason she'd fled in the first place. He'd put the part about the hotel in his note so she'd know he didn't expect her to fall into bed with him every minute of her stay.

He hadn't wanted to apologize for what had been a glorious event. Their lovemaking had meant everything to him. The feeling of oneness, the emotional commitment. But they hadn't talked, and until they did, he didn't want her to think it had just been sex and nothing else.

Obviously a note hadn't been the right approach to take.

She'd left.

"Please let her forgive me," he whispered in prayer.

The pilot's voice came over the intercom. "We'll be landing in ten minutes. Please fasten your seat belts."

His was already fastened. He'd been ready since he got on the plane.

All he had was a carry-on bag. He'd have to return to Chicago, of course, to pack everything up, but he hadn't wanted anything to slow him down today. Standing at the baggage claim for half an hour wouldn't be something he could tolerate.

At his meeting earlier today, he'd told his boss he was leaving the firm. It was flattering that the man had appeared upset and offered him an increase in salary if he'd stay, but Russ had declined.

His boss had asked him to meet with him again on Monday to discuss his decision. Russ had agreed, thinking he'd be in Chicago. Now he didn't know when he'd go back. It depended on Melissa. He wasn't leaving until they'd settled their difficulties.

And he was coming back for good as soon as possible.

He'd been financially responsible since he'd gotten his first job, saving and making investments. He had considerable resources, plus his vested pension with the company. He was well-prepared for the change in his life.

There had been a lot of changes since he'd first come back to Wyoming. The call from his mother on Thursday was a major one. He'd spent the rest of the day getting to know the woman who'd left him at the Lost Springs Ranch.

And her husband and two children.

He had two half sisters, fifteen and seventeen. They seemed well-adjusted, happy teenagers. His stepfather was a good man. He'd met Russ's mother,

Emily, after she'd pulled her life together, gone back to school and then taken a job as a secretary.

Before they'd married, she'd told him about giving up her son. He had offered to help her find Russ, to adopt him, but she'd refused.

Melissa had been right. His mother had suffered for her actions. She'd believed she didn't have the right to interfere in his life again, and she'd punished herself ever since she'd abandoned her son.

Russ and his mother hadn't wiped out the pain of those years, but they'd made a start. And he intended to keep in touch. Of course, he wouldn't be living in Chicago now, but he would visit. And he would invite them to Wyoming.

He'd intended to share all that had happened with Melissa. To thank her for leading him toward that reconciliation. To introduce her to his new family.

The plane touched down on the tarmac and he stowed away all those thoughts. It was time to focus on Melissa. Time to organize his thoughts, to prepare an apology. It was time to come home.

He had to be patient when the crowds began making their way off the plane. An older lady needed assistance getting a huge carry-on bag down from the overhead bin. He handled it easily and carried it up the aisle for her. It was faster that way.

When they reached the terminal, he thankfully handed it to her son and strode through the airport at a speed just short of an all-out run. He had the back door of the taxi open before the driver even saw him.

Once he'd given the driver the address, it was all he could do not to urge the man to speed. But he wanted to get there safely.

When the cab came to a stop, he shoved money into the driver's hand, grabbed his bag and got out, muttering a hasty thanks over his shoulder. Then he raced for the front door of Melissa's house.

Finally, he was here.

MELISSA HAD SPENT the afternoon working through her depression. She had to get over this silliness. There had never been a future with Russ. She'd known that.

So why was she feeling so bereft, as if someone had died?

Was it because her unreasonable hopes and dreams had crashed? Maybe they needed a respectful burial, she decided. "I wonder if I should order a wreath," she muttered at the bizarre thought.

Strangely enough, she felt a certain sympathy for the woman on the phone. She, too, would be heart-broken when she discovered Russ had slept with Melissa.

If she found out. Maybe Russ intended something permanent with the other woman. That thought was painful, too. But then everything was today.

Mandy was down for her nap and Melissa had put in a load of clothes to wash. She'd already cleaned her little house. She didn't have any paperwork to do for the office. What was she going to do now?

She began pacing her living room, trying to blank

out her thoughts, but she wasn't successful. She re-
lived the time in Russ's arms minute by agonizing
minute, a terrible longing filling her.

It took several knocks on her door before she realized someone was there. Expecting Mrs. Tuttle, she
swung it open without hesitation.

"Russ," she gasped. Then tried to close the door
in his face.

He would have none of it.

Grabbing the door, he forced it back and stepped
inside. For a moment they simply stared at each
other.

"What are you doing here?" She tried to make
her voice sound firm, in control, but the words came
out weak and whispery.

"We need to talk."

Oh dear. Her heart sank. He must have realized
she'd found out about the other woman. Was he going to tell her the woman didn't matter to him? That
he'd just "had sex" the night before she got to town?

"No! There's no need. I don't want to discuss it."

He stepped closer and she moved back. "But if
we don't discuss it, how can we work things out?"

"We can't," she muttered bleakly, shifting her
gaze from his face. It hurt too much to look at him.
"I made a mistake. I'll deal with it."

He grabbed her shoulder. "It wasn't a mistake,
Melissa. It was—it was wonderful! Look, I know I
rushed you, but I promise I won't make that mistake
again. You can have more time. After—"

"No!" She wrenched herself from his hold and

turned her back on him. "Is that what you told her, too?"

He said nothing, and it was all Melissa could do not to turn and see if he looked as guilty as she imagined him to be.

"Her?" he finally asked.

Now she did turn around. She couldn't end this like a coward. And she had to end it. "Please, Russ, don't bother lying. I was there when she called."

"Who called? What are you talking about?" He truly sounded bewildered, but she wasn't going to fall for that. Not after hearing the woman's voice.

"I don't know her name. She didn't leave it in the message. I'm sure she thought you'd know who it was since you'd obviously been together the night before." After a big gulp of air, she added, "She probably didn't realize how busy you've been."

He frowned, as if still trying to figure out who had called. "Look, Melissa, I'm not in high school. I never said I haven't had other lovers. But there hasn't been anyone recently. Certainly not since I spent time with you and Mandy."

She laughed, her voice cracking. "Right!" And she'd thought him an honest man, if nothing else.

"Is this woman's call the reason you left? You weren't upset that we made love last night?"

"It doesn't matter anymore, Russ. It's over. I just want you to leave."

"No, I won't. What we have is important, Melissa. I won't give up without a fight."

She stared at him, still loving the look of him, his

strength, his determination, the passion in his gaze. "There'll be no fight, Russ. You see, you've already tripped yourself up. The woman said she was with you Thursday night, not weeks or months ago. The night before I arrived." She closed her eyes and turned away from him. "She said she loves you! As much as I—"

"Whoever she was, she was lying," Russ assured her, pulling her back against his broad chest, holding her there. "And I can prove it."

"No, you can't. Even if the date is wrong, I heard it in her voice, Russ! She loves you, desperately!"

"What exactly did she say?" he suddenly asked, a strange note in his voice.

"I—I don't remember." She wasn't about to repeat that damning message to him. "Didn't you check your messages before you left?"

"Why would I? You were the only person I wanted to hear from and you wrote me a note. A damned note that said absolutely nothing." Abruptly, he released her and walked past her to the kitchen.

Surprised, she followed, reaching the room in time to see him dialing the phone. "What are you doing?"

"Retrieving my messages."

She pulled out a chair and sat down at the table, uncertain whether her trembling legs would hold her up. She sneaked a look at his face, expecting to see consternation, at the very least, at being caught. Instead, he was smiling.

He hung up the phone and turned to look at her,

a strange expression on his face. "Were you about to say the woman loved me as much as you do?"

Her face turned a bright red, but she wasn't about to make that confession.

"I hope it isn't the same kind of love. I don't want you for a mother."

His words didn't pierce through her misery for several minutes. She stared at his smile, unable to comprehend what could be causing it. Then her gaze sharpened. "Mother? You don't—I mean, you don't know where your mother is."

"Yes, I do. I was going to tell you last night, but we got a little distracted."

"What? You've talked to your mother?"

"My mother, my stepfather, my two half sisters. They're pretty girls. You'll like them."

He continued watching her as his words sank in. He had found his family. It had been his mother on the phone. Melissa thought through the words the woman had said, trying them out as a mother's message rather than a lover's.

"I don't believe you."

"I'm going to call Chicago, if that's what it takes, but I'll pay for the call," he said calmly, picking up the phone and dialing a number.

Why was he acting so strangely? she wondered. Why would he suddenly call Chicago?

"Mother? It's Russ," he said when the connection went through. "Thanks for calling. Thursday night was great for me, too."

She froze. Could it really be true?

"No, I can't. I'm in Wyoming." He paused, then said, "Yeah, that's her. I couldn't stay away. Would you like to say hi?" He turned and held out the phone. "Say hi to my mother, Emily Blackman."

Still staring at him, Melissa took the phone. "Hello?"

"Melissa, I'm so pleased to at least talk to you. Russ told us all about you Thursday night. I'm so grateful you encouraged him to contact me."

"I—it was nothing."

"No, my dear, it was everything. I've been torturing myself for almost thirty years. Now my life is truly happy."

"I'm glad," she murmured, feeling terrible. "Here's Russ, Mrs. Blackman." She handed the phone back to him and fought the urge to hide while he finished his conversation. But she couldn't do that. He'd probably never speak to her again after her ugly accusations.

He hung up the phone and turned to face her. "Did you recognize her voice?"

She nodded, licking her suddenly dry lips. "I'm sorry. I assumed—"

"Tell me you love me."

Only the demand. No assurances on his part, no promises, not even a smile.

But she owed him honesty.

"I love you."

With a whoop of celebration, he lifted her into his arms, his lips greeting hers with the kiss she'd feared would never be hers again.

When he finally released her, too soon in her opinion, he asked, "Do you believe I love you?"

"Yes," she whispered.

"And Mandy? Do you believe I love Mandy?"

She nodded.

"Then I suggest we find the closest spot to tie the knot, Melissa Bright, before I take you to bed again."

She desperately wanted the same thing, but there was her business, her home. She wasn't an eighteen-year-old starting out fresh. "But Chicago—"

"We'll visit occasionally."

"Russ, I can't just pack up and leave. My company—"

"Chicago. We'll visit Chicago occasionally. To see my family. I can't turn my back on my mother now."

"No, of course not, but your job—"

"I resigned this morning."

"Before you came back to the apartment?"

"Yeah."

"Oh, Russ..." She reached out for him and he didn't hesitate. He wrapped his arms around her and kissed her with all the love in him.

A plaintive wail interrupted them. "Mandy's awake," Melissa announced.

As she started toward the baby's room, Russ caught her arm. "Let me," he said.

Knowing how much Mandy would enjoy Russ's attention, Melissa stood back to let him by, then followed him down the hall.

When he entered the room, the baby fell silent. As he reached for her, however, she squealed and bounced on her toes. "Da-da-da-da!"

"Yes, sweetheart, Daddy's here."

Melissa's heart melted at his words. She and Mandy were very fortunate. They'd found a man who loved both of them. She stood on tiptoes to kiss his cheek, but he turned his head and kissed her solidly on the lips.

Mandy patted his cheek and babbled, "Ma-ma-ma-ma!"

He pulled back. "Is your daughter protesting or encouraging us?"

"I don't know," she said, laughing, but her voice was trembly.

"Will I lose any brownie points if I put her in her playpen?"

She shook her head no.

Russ took the baby to the living room and sat her down, in spite of her protest. Drawing Melissa back into his embrace, he covered her lips with his. He didn't ever want to let her go.

When he began unbuttoning her shirt, her hand covered his. "Russ, we can't. Mandy."

"Oh, yeah," he agreed with a huff of frustration. "And I guess I wasn't keeping my promise, anyway. I said I'd be patient."

"I think patience is highly overrated," she murmured, a smile on her lips that had him reaching for her again.

"When does Mandy take a nap?" he asked, his voice rough with desire.

"She's already had her nap."

"So we have to wait until she goes to sleep?"

Melissa nodded.

"Then you'd better take me to a hotel."

Stunned, she stared at him, then noticed the teasing glint in his eyes. "Oh, no you don't. That offer's withdrawn. You're staying right here. We'll be frustrated together—until Mandy goes to bed."

He pulled her close for another drugging kiss. "Okay," he agreed. "If you're sure."

"I'm sure. I love you, Russ."

His heart leaped. He hadn't realized how much he'd longed to hear those words.

"I love you, too. More than I'd ever thought possible." Again he kissed her, a kiss that promised everlasting love. "I've made a lot of plans," he told her.

"You have?"

"Yeah. I'm going to start my own firm here in Casper. And I'm going to build that house you loved."

She drew back. "You are?"

He nodded. "For you and me and Mandy. And any other babies that come along." His hand slid to her stomach. "Do you want other babies?"

"Oh, yes. I never wanted Mandy to be an only child. And I'd love to have your baby. If you want us to."

"I'd feel like the luckiest man in the world, sweetheart. Mandy and I want all the babies we can get."

"Mandy does? How do you know?"

"Because I was alone, like her."

"Me, too."

"Good. Then what do you say we work on that little project tonight?"

"Good idea," she agreed.

He led her to the couch and settled her on his lap. They had another couple of hours before Mandy went to sleep, and he intended to get all the talking that needed to be done out of the way.

He planned to be busy later.

Thank God his bachelor days were over.

EPILOGUE

Russ and Mandy were in the den, stacking building blocks, while they waited for Melissa to get up from her nap. He'd insisted she lie down each afternoon now that she was so big with his child.

"Russ?" Her voice drifted down from upstairs.

"Yeah, sweetheart, I'm coming." He scooped up Mandy, much to her delight, and hurried up the stairs. They'd been in their new house for three months now. He'd hurried the construction so they could move in before Melissa got too far along in her pregnancy.

He entered the bedroom, a smile on his face. These days he smiled all the time.

Then he frowned. "What's wrong?"

"Mommy?" Mandy said, echoing his worried tone.

"I'm okay," Melissa assured them both, "but I think it's time."

Russ froze. He'd prepared for this day, taking classes with Melissa, reading books. But now the time had come, he felt a sudden panic. "You mean you're in labor?"

"Yes. Call Natalie and then the doctor."

She'd written those two numbers by every phone in the house. He'd teased her about it, but now he was glad. He couldn't remember either one.

Natalie had moved to Casper to live with Mrs. Tuttle shortly after their wedding. She'd promised to come care for Mandy when the baby arrived.

"Natalie? It's Russ. It's time. Can you come right away?"

As soon as she agreed, he dialed the doctor's number. "Dr. Pelham, it's Russ Hall. Melissa's in labor." He turned to his wife. "He wants to know how far apart the contractions are."

"About six minutes. I've been feeling some discomfort since this morning."

"Why didn't you tell me?" he demanded, hurt that she'd kept it from him.

"Because you would've wanted to go to the hospital right away, and it wasn't time," she said calmly, a smile on her face.

He expelled a deep breath of frustration and repeated the information to the doctor. After receiving instructions, he hung up the phone. "Come on. We're supposed to go to the hospital at once."

"I know. Will you forgive me?"

He stood Mandy on the floor and drew Melissa into his arms. "I just want to protect you, sweetheart."

"You do, Russ. Mandy and I are so well-protected and loved. We couldn't be happier."

"Me, neither," he assured her before his lips covered hers. The kiss was ended when he felt her muscles tighten with another contraction.

He turned and headed for the stairs. "Come on, Mandy," he called, not forgetting the little girl who'd taught him about babies.

"Okay, Daddy," she agreed, grabbing his pant leg.

"Can you walk? he asked Melissa. "I'm afraid to leave Mandy to navigate the stairs by herself."

Melissa agreed, but Mandy had no fear. She was already several steps down.

"Wait, Mandy. I'll carry you," he assured her. Once he'd carried her down, he hurried back to help Melissa. By the time she reached the bottom of the stairs, Mandy was on her way back up.

"Mandy, come back," he called, going after her. "I never should've built a two-story house," he muttered.

"The house is perfect, Russ."

He returned to her side for another kiss, Mandy struggling in his arms to get free.

He raised his mouth from hers reluctantly. "If her brother is half as active as Mandy, I'm going to become skin and bones. I can't keep up with her."

Melissa grabbed his arm as another contraction seized her. "I—I think they're getting closer together."

"Yeah," he agreed, worry filling him. The sound of a car had him running to the window. "Natalie is here. We'll be at the hospital in a few minutes, sweetheart."

He opened the door for their friend, handed Mandy over to her and guided Melissa out of the house.

"Oh, my suitcase. It's in the hall closet," Melissa reminded him.

He ran back in, grabbed the suitcase, kissed Mandy goodbye and raced to the car.

As he drove to the hospital, he once again counted his blessings. "You know, if our son ever wants to be in a bachelor auction," he began, reaching over to pat her stomach, "I'm going to be all in favor of it."

Melissa smiled. "Me, too."

Russ pulled her closer, driving with one hand. "You okay?"

"Yes, I'm fine. But I'm in a hurry to meet the next Hall bachelor. I only hope he'll be as perfect as his father."

"I just hope he'll be as lucky," Russ said, and turned into the hospital parking lot.

HEART OF THE WEST

continues with

THE BEST MAN IN WYOMING

by

Margot Dalton

Lindsay Duncan had hastily proposed a camping trip
with some of the boys from the ranch, and she
wanted—needed—Rex Trowbridge to accompany
them. Could elegant Rex even ride a horse
anymore? Could he stand to spend days on end
sleeping under the stars with her and six high-
spirited boys? Could he stop teasing her long
enough to recognize what was really simmering
between the two of them—and do something about
it before it was too late?

Available in June

Here's a preview!

"YOU'RE GOING to need a tent," Rex said with an authoritative edge to his voice that probably worked really well around his office. "The boys can sleep out, and so can I. But I want you, at least, to have some privacy."

"Why?"

Rex leaned back and set the papers down at his side. He laced his fingers behind his head and stared through the window at the stable, where Clint Kraft's lanky figure could be seen among a group of horses.

"These kids aren't little boys, Lindsay," he said. "And you're a very pretty lady. Believe me," he added with a grin, "I can remember what it was like to be fifteen. So I think it will be more comfortable for everybody if you're sleeping and dressing inside a tent."

She thought it over, reluctant to give in. "In the past, I've always slept out on the ground with the boys and there's never been a problem."

"But those are younger boys who go on the little weekend campouts," Rex pointed out. "And this time we'll be gone for over a week. Just listen to me, Lindsay, and try not to argue for once in your life. I know what I'm talking about.''

Though she hated to admit it, he was probably right. Lindsay said nothing, but she jotted a reminder to herself about checking into available dome tents in the supply room.

"Besides," Rex added casually, studying a scuffed area on the side of his leather boot, "what if you have company some night?"

"Company?" she asked, still thinking about the supply room. "What kind of company?"

"Overnight company." His eyes rested on her with unmistakable meaning. "It would certainly be best to keep a visit like that private, wouldn't it, Lin?"

"Look, I have..." Annoyingly her voice caught and squeaked. She had to clear her throat and start again while he kept watching her intently. "I have no idea what you're talking about," she concluded with all the dignity she could muster.

"No idea at all, Linnie?"

She put the pen down and sat erect, folding her hands tightly on the desk in front of her. "I don't think you have this all straight yet, Rex," she said. "There will be no visitors in my tent on this camping trip. It's not going to happen. Do you understand?"

"But what if poor little Danny has a nightmare?" Rex's eyes sparkled with laughter.

"Then Danny would come into the tent and sleep with me, and bring his teddy bear," Lindsay said. "But he's eight years old. Anybody older than eight can spend the night outdoors."

"Even if one of the bigger guys has a nightmare?" Rex asked, his face deliberately sober, though his eyes continued to dance. "Like for instance, what if the biggest guy of all has a really bad dream, and needs some comforting in the middle of the night? Would you be coldhearted and turn him away, Lin?"

"In an instant," she said. But her heart was pounding, her whole body moist with yearning as she pictured the deep shadowed woods, the starry blackness overhead, the scent of pine and the sleeping boys sprawled all around dying embers of a wood fire.

And Rex slipping silently into her tent in the moonlight, lying with her on the rumpled bedroll, holding her and kissing her, their naked bodies warm as fire in the chill of the night...

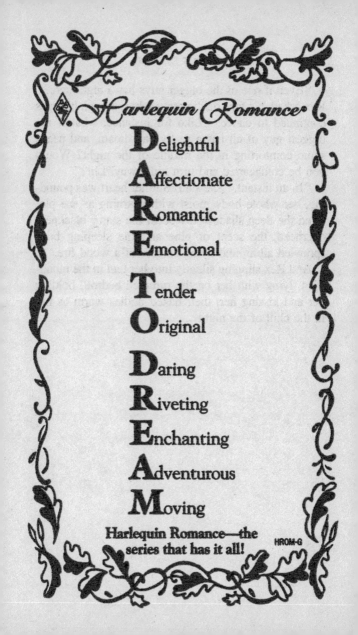

Harlequin Romance

Delightful

Affectionate

Romantic

Emotional

Tender

Original

Daring

Riveting

Enchanting

Adventurous

Moving

Harlequin Romance—the
series that has it all!

HROM-G

HARLEQUIN PRESENTS®

HARLEQUIN PRESENTS
men you won't be able to resist
falling in love with...

HARLEQUIN PRESENTS
women who have feelings
just like your own...

HARLEQUIN PRESENTS
powerful passion in
exotic international settings...

HARLEQUIN PRESENTS
intense, dramatic stories that will keep you
turning to the very last page...

HARLEQUIN PRESENTS
The world's bestselling romance series!

PRES-G

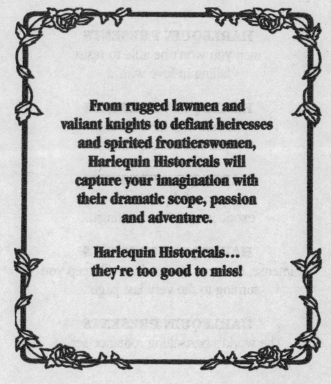

From rugged lawmen and
valiant knights to defiant heiresses
and spirited frontierswomen,
Harlequin Historicals will
capture your imagination with
their dramatic scope, passion
and adventure.

Harlequin Historicals...
they're too good to miss!

HHGENR

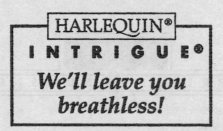

LOOK FOR OUR FOUR FABULOUS MEN!

Each month some of today's bestselling authors bring
four new fabulous men to Harlequin American Romance.
Whether they're rebel ranchers, millionaire power brokers
or sexy single dads, they're all gallant princes—and
they're all ready to sweep you into lighthearted fantasies
and contemporary fairy tales where anything is possible
and where all your dreams come true!

You don't even have to make a wish...
Harlequin American Romance will grant your every desire!

Look for Harlequin American Romance
wherever Harlequin books are sold!